ROARING RANGE

**Center Point
Large Print**

**This Large Print Book carries the
Seal of Approval of N.A.V.H.**

ROARING RANGE

L. P. HOLMES

CENTER POINT PUBLISHING
THORNDIKE, MAINE

This Center Point Large Print edition
is published in the year 2005 by arrangement with
Golden West Literary Agency.

The text of this Large Print edition is unabridged. In other
aspects, this book may vary from the original edition. Printed in
Thailand. Set in 16-point Times New Roman type.

ISBN 1-58547-673-0

Library of Congress Cataloging-in-Publication Data

Holmes, L. P. (Llewellyn Perry), 1895-
    Roaring range / L. P. Holmes.--Center Point large print ed.
      p. cm.
    ISBN 1-58547-673-0 (lib. bdg. : alk. paper)
    1. Large type books. I. Title.

PS3515.O4448R63 2005
813'.52--dc22

                                                          2005014330

ROARING RANGE

I

THE GROUP OF MEN WHO HAD BEEN MILLING ANXIOUSLY in front of the Algerine Saloon and Gambling Hall, had suddenly tensed and quieted. Every eye among them turned to the man who had just stepped into view through the swinging doors.

The individual in question was tall, well built and moved with a graceful, cultured ease. His skin was swarthy; his eyes black, and the dark hair on his uncovered head was combed and brushed to a sleek brilliance.

He was carefully and expensively dressed in a store suit of black serge with a white silk shirt and a flowing, four-in-hand tie of subdued shade. His only concession to the customs of the country lay in the expensive, high-heeled riding boots and the bulk of a shoulder-holstered gun.

"Gentlemen," he announced in a soft, slightly sibilant voice, "I wish to thank you. The voters of Rhyolite County have elected me their sheriff by a majority of fourteen votes."

A strange medley of hoarse cheers and curses of disgust answered this statement. Some of the crowd pushed forward noisily, to close about the speaker and shake his hand. Others moved back, saying little, while their faces turned grim and hostile.

A second man appeared in the doorway; an elderly

man, rather gaunt, with a square-jawed, seamed face, graying hair and mustache and deep-set, steady blue eyes. As he started to push through the crowd the swarthy speaker laid a hand on his arm.

"You are offering me your congratulations of course, Raine?" he suggested.

The elderly cattleman stared for a moment, then shook his arm free. "I'm offerin' yuh nothin', Partridge," he rumbled in a deep, resonant voice. "Yuh got nothin' to be congratulated for. That election was a farce. Yuh know it—I know it, an' everybody else in the county is due to find it out inside the next week.

"If yuh think it represents the desire of the majority yuh're badly mistaken, an' yuh're due to find it out the first time yuh pull one of the off-color tricks I know yuh're figgerin' on. It was a plain, up an' down steal, engineered by yore money an' the worthless crowd yuh've got workin' with yuh.

"One thing yuh want to remember, Partridge. The law is law only as long as it's fair. After that it's persecution. An' I'm warnin' yuh—the people of Rhyolite County won't stand for persecution. But here is the star an' there's the office across the street. Take 'em both an' do yore damndest."

Jay Partridge smiled; a superior, slightly mocking smile as he accepted the badge of office. "That talk smacks a lot of sour grapes, Raine. Don't flatter yourself. Other folks besides you are perfectly able to administer the law of Rhyolite County. I'm not holding you to your insulting inferences, for I make allowance

8

for your natural feelings of disappointment and cha-grin on being defeated."

While speaking thus, Partridge had let his left hand play a moment about the carefully built knot of his tie. It was a careless, perfectly natural gesture; yet one of the crowd, upon observing it, pushed close against Bill Raine's right elbow.

"Better go slow on that kinda talk, Raine," growled this fellow, a short, spidery built puncher with tow hair, pale, unwinking eyes and a tight, narrow slit of a mouth. "I was one of those who worked for Mr. Par-tridge, an' when yuh say the election was pulled crooked yuh're steppin' on my toes. Which ain't sup-posed to be healthy in these parts."

Bill Raine turned and looked down into those pale eyes. He laughed contemptuously. "A human hyena leads the pack an' the jackals bark and chatter. Yuh're not tryin' to scare me, are yuh, Evans?"

Claude Evans drew slightly back and his thin shoul-ders settled in a queer, tense hunch. "I'm not tryin' to scare yuh—no, Raine. I'm just warnin' yuh to go slow on the kinda talk yuh're dishin' out. It ain't healthy."

For a man of his age, Bill Raine moved with startling swiftness. His left hand shot down and gripped the viperish little gunman's right wrist. His own big, right hand, muscular and calloused, smacked like a hard-swung board against Evans' face. Evans slumped down in a heap.

A rising snarl rose through the crowd. They swung away in a rough circle, leaving Raine standing alone and in the clear above the fallen, dazed gunman. Stooping, Raine twitched the gun from Evans' side and began idly punching the fat, yellow, deadly shells from it.

"I reckon that's my answer to a mealy-mouthed dry-gulcher an' sneak-thief," he rumbled steadily. He looked over his shoulder with a contemptuous laugh. "Take him, Partridge. He's one of yore pack."

A gun lock clicked ominously from behind him. He turned slowly, his face harsh and set. Then a new voice broke in from beyond the edge of the crowd—a soft, drawling voice that was almost apologetic, but the crowd relaxed and quieted as it came.

"Don't any of yuh gents forget that me an' Early are on deck. On deck an' backin' the boss to a finish."

Two punchers moved carelessly through the crush and stood beside Raine. They were both tall, slender fellows with leathery faces and steady eyes. Both were roughly dressed in worn range togs and both wore two guns, tied down.

Raine chuckled affectionately. "That air-tight, Texas combination of Lon Sheer an' Jim Early are present an' ready to oblige, it seems. Anybody got anythin' more to say?"

Apparently no one had. Raine looked at Jay Partridge, the new sheriff of Rhyolite County. Partridge was still standing, easily posed in the doorway of the Algerine. Apparently he was, if anything, but slightly amused at what had happened. Yet a careful observer would have noted that Partridge's nostrils were quivering and his eyes were nothing more than a glitter of hard, surface lights.

Raine laughed again, then pushed his way out of the crowd and up the street. Jim Early and Lon Sheer moved along beside him, silent, slouching, and yet somehow terribly potent.

"I reckon the lid's off now, boss," drawled Sheer.

Raine nodded. "I was afraid of it, Lon. We've got dark times ahead. The ole Lincoln County War ain't a flea bite to what Rhyolite County is haided for. This range will be painted with blood. Partridge has got what he's been workin' for a long time. He an' his crowd will strip this country to the bone. Yeah, there's trouble ahead—plenty of it."

"I cain't figger yet how he won, Bill," said Jim Early.

Raine laughed bitterly. "There'll be a lot of folks wonderin' how it happened, Jim. I can tell 'em. Over-confidence was one reason; over-confidence by a lot of smug, pig-haided ranchers who wouldn't listen to reason. I watched close, an' there wasn't a single vote cast by the whole H Bar O Connected outfit.

"They never showed at all. They didn't vote against me, neither did they vote for me. Well, reckon I better drop into Hoskins' place an' break the bad news to Norma. It'll hurt her. She's been mighty proud of her ole dad."

They turned in through the shadowy doorway of a typical, range country general store. As they entered a slender, brown-haired girl in divided, corduroy skirts, blue woolen blouse and riding boots came running up out of the cool gloom. "How much did you win by, Dad?" she cried.

Bill Raine was silent a moment, while he tucked a fatherly arm about her waist. He shook his head. "I didn't win, honey. Partridge licked me by fourteen votes."

"What?" The girl stiffened and looked at her father searchingly. "You're trying to tease me. Of course you won."

Raine shrugged. "I'm not teasin' yuh, Norma. I saw the votes counted. Partridge won."

Weazened-up, whiskery Ezra Hoskins, the store-keeper, came shuffling excitedly forward. "Bill," he piped nasally, "yuh don't mean that?"

"I do mean it, Ezry. I'm not a sheriff any more. I'm just a plain, hard-workin' cattleman."

"Well, consarn my hide," yelped the storekeeper. "If that ain't a disgrace to this county. That no-good, slick-talking, gamblin', dive-runnin', Jay Partridge posin' as a sheriff. What's the world comin' to?"

"Comin' to blood an' fire an' thievery, Ezry," rumbled Raine. "I want to use yore big storeroom tonight, Ezry. I'm callin' a mass meetin' of all the biggest ranchers. I'm gonna try an' make 'em see the light.

"We gotta combine if we expect to fight off the element that's gonna start workin' on this range. Partridge is organized. He showed that today by winnin' the election. He's got bigger idees than just runnin' that Algerine dump of his. He's out to own this range, to control it—lock, stock an' barrel."

12

"The room's yores, Bill," declared Hoskins. "That an' anythin' else I own. Jay Partridge, sheriff! Hell's heat! Did yuh ever hear of such a crazy idee?"

"Thanks, Ezry," said Raine. "If half the folks in Rhyolite County had yore gumption, this'd be a white man's paradise."

Raine turned to his loyal punchers. "Jim and Lon, hit yore saddles an' spread the news, will yuh? Get in touch with Gaston, Ryan, Batten, Harding, Orcutt an' any of the others yuh happen to run across. But be shore an' get them I named. Tell 'em eight o'clock tonight, here at Ezry's store."

Lon Sheer and Jim Early nodded and moved toward the door. "Oh yeah," called Raine. "I nearly forgot. Be shore an' get that new owner of the Fishhook spread. I wanta find just where that jasper stands, too."

Lon and Jim disappeared into the white heat of the sunshine and presently flashed across the vista offered by the open door, riding swiftly. Raine turned to his daughter, Norma, who had been standing still and downcast beside him.

Bill sensed that there were tears in the girl's eyes. He patted her shoulder gently. "There—there, honey. Don't yuh go to feelin' bad. I ain't weepin' no tears about this thing. A man cain't expect to hold office forever."

"It isn't that," flared the girl suddenly. "If your opponent had been a decent, law-abiding citizen I would be the first to congratulate him. But to think that Jay Partridge—with all he represents—should be voted into

13

office over your head, when you've worked so hard for the county and done such good work. . . . Well, it just makes me want to swear and rail like a mule skinner."

Raine chuckled, but the chuckle broke off as a third figure advanced leisurely from the wilderness of supplies which filled the big room to overflowing. He was dangling a new bridle in one big hand.

"Find what yuh want?" snapped Hoskins, so upset by the news he had heard that he didn't care whether he made a sale or not.

"Yeah," came the quiet, easy drawl. "This suits me. The tag says sixteen dollars. Put it on the books against the Fishhook Ranch."

Raine stiffened and slowly turned, squinting his deep-set eyes as he tried to take in the looks of this stranger. Though the stranger's features were hardly distinguishable from the shadow, Raine sensed a lean, strongly cast face—stern-jawed and masterful.

In stature the fellow was fairly tall, wide and flat of shoulder with the lean flanks of the rider. A faded hickory shirt clung snugly about the muscular torso and a pair of worn, wide-skirted batwing chaps fluttered as he walked. He carried one gun, slung low and slightly to the front of the right thigh.

Suddenly the young fellow turned to Raine. "Beggin' yore pardon, amigo," he drawled. "I couldn't help overhearin' what yuh told yore two men a minute ago. I'm Cole Bridger, boss of the Fishhook spread. Did I understand yuh as wantin' me to be present in this store tonight?"

Raine nodded. "I'm Bill Raine. Yeah, I was hopin' yuh'd come around. It'll be for yore own benefit. I may be all wrong, of course. But it looks to me like the time is here for the substantial citizens of this range to sort of get together in mutual protection. And, shore, it won't cost nothin' to talk things over."

"I take it yuh don't think a heap of this new crowd that's just gone into power."

Raine laughed. "Yuh're shore enough a stranger in these parts, Bridger, or yuh wouldn't have to ask that question. When a professional gambler, killer an' dive-keeper haids a county's politics, what's the answer?"

Bridger smiled slightly. "A case of write yore own ticket, I reckon."

A small, insistent hand was jabbing Bill Raine in the ribs. Suddenly he understood. "Oh shore," he rumbled. "Bridger, let me make yuh acquainted with my daughter, Norma. She's at once my blessin' an' cross. I know I cain't get along without her an' there's times when I have a devil of a time gettin' along with her."

Norma stepped forward and put out a slim, brown little hand. "I'm glad to know you, Mr. Bridger," she smiled. "Don't mind Dad. He always gets mad at me when I make him shave and put on a clean shirt."

Bridger cradled that outstretched hand in his own muscular paw and sensed a distinctly pleasurable thrill at the contact. He chuckled boyishly, and Norma caught a gleam of even, white teeth.

"I'm happy to know yuh, Miss Raine. Yuh just keep on rawhidin' yore daddy whenever yuh feel that way.

Bein' a man, an' understandin' the ornery critters pretty well, I know that a little rawhidin' is good for the soul of them, now an' then. An' shore, he seems to be standin' up under the persecution all right."

Raine rumbled with soft laughter. "Yuh're callin' the turn pretty close, Bridger."

Old Bill Raine felt unaccountably warmed to this young stranger. Bridger seemed every inch a man, quick of mind and facile of wit. As for Norma, she studied Bridger with inscrutable eyes and concluded that she approved very decidedly of him. There was a clean, lithe, easy strength and grace about him that was distinctly appealing.

They chatted lightly for another minute or two and then Raine turned toward the door. "Reckon we might as well amble on out to the ranch, honey," he told Norma. "Thank the Lord I'll be able to settle down to the business of honest cattle raisin' again.

"I won't have to be bargin' all around the country any more, tryin' to straighten out other folks' troubles. The more I think it over the more I'm gettin' to feel relieved that I was beat in that election. I can mind my own business for a change."

The three of them emerged into the white sun blaze and Cole Bridger seized upon this opportunity to take a guarded, but thorough survey of Norma Raine's indubitable charms. He decided that her slightly wavy brown hair was light enough in color to be called blond.

Her eyes were vividly blue and shaded with long,

curling lashes. Her nose was straight and sensitive of nostril. Her mouth was generous in size, but winsomely curved and of scarlet purity. Her face, slightly oval, tapered to a well set, determined little chin.

There was a hint of a ready dimple in her right cheek. Her skin was like sun-browned ivory with a powdering of freckles across the bridge of her nose. She was of average height, slim and muscular; as she walked, she moved with the free, flowing grace of perfect health.

Norma was well aware of Cole Bridger's scrutiny, but it did not displease her. For some strange reason she wanted very much to impress him favorably.

It happened that all three of their horses were tied to the same hitching-rail, with which both sides of the single street of the town of Baird were lined. "If yuh don't mind," suggested Bridger, as he hung his new bridle over his saddle horn, "I'll ride along with you folks. My way home leads out a couple of miles along yore trail."

"Shore," nodded Raine. "Glad to have yuh, Bridger."

Norma smiled her welcome also, a welcome that quickened Cole's blood. They were in a little group as they unhitched their horses and Bridger, getting his free first, threw a casual glance down the street toward the Algerine Saloon. For a fractional second he tensed, then acted quickly.

With a strong, but gentle sweep of his arm he literally tossed Norma beyond the bulk of the horses. Whirling, he struck Bill Raine with the full impact of his body, sending the old cattleman plunging forward on his hands and knees. Then he leaped clear of the entire group, whipping out his gun as he did so.

Bill Raine, amazed and bewildered, started to curse, but broke off sharply as a bullet whimpered past his head, gouging into the hitching-rail and sending a cloud of splinters flying. Down the street a gun bayed heavily. The answer came from Cole Bridger, who flung two lightning shots from his hip as he crouched, strung tight and cold-eyed.

A gasping yell emanated from the mouth of the alley on the far side of the Algerine Saloon. From that alley a man came staggering, a wispy, spidery-looking individual. His head was back and both hands were clawing at the base of his throat. He weaved drunkenly, stumbling over invisible obstacles. Abruptly he lurched forward on his face, where he writhed a moment, then lay still.

Several men plunged from the doorway of the Algerine, running for the fallen man. Cole Bridger holstered his gun and walked quietly to meet them. Jay Partridge appeared in the doorway of his saloon, paused a moment, then pushed up to the ever thickening crowd that was gathering around the dead man.

"It's Evans—Claude Evans," vociferated one of the crowd. "He's daid as a mackerel, plugged square through the throat. An' here's the jasper who salivated him."

Cole felt the impact of hard, calculating looks, but he did not hesitate. He elbowed his way up to the man he had shot and across him faced the black, unwinking eyes of Jay Partridge.

"Is that right?" snapped Partridge. "Did you kill this man?"

A chill flicker grew and deepened in Cole's glance. "Yeah, I did," he drawled. "What's it to yuh?"

Partridge's lips thinned. "You're talking to the newly elected sheriff of Rhyolite County, fellow," he warned. "Don't try and get hard. It won't pay."

Cole laughed. "Somehow I ain't one mite scared," he mocked. "Sheriff or no sheriff, whenever I catch a sneakin' dry-gulcher about to try his stuff I rock him off like I would a coiled diamond-back. What's eatin' yuh? Is that jasper a pet friend of yores?"

There was no mistaking the contemptuous meaning of Cole's words. Partridge's right hand began to steal upward toward the left lapel of his immaculate coat. Cole hooked his thumb through his gunbelt, not far from the worn butt of his heavy gun. "I wouldn't try it, was I you," he murmured quietly. "I know yuh got a gun in a shoulder holster. But yuh cain't begin to get it out fast enough."

For a tense moment their glances locked and then Partridge's hand fell away. "I'm holding you of course," he snapped. "You're under arrest until you can prove the truth of your claim."

The crowd split apart as Bill Raine came charging through in time to hear Partridge's words. "Proof be damned!" roared the irate old cattleman. "If it's proof yuh want, come on over here an' I'll show yuh where

19

Evans' bullet didn't miss me by the width of a cat's whisker.

"He was tryin' to pot me from that alley. His slug like to of tore the hitchin'-rail in half. The yellow, back-bitin' whelp got what was comin' to him."

Partridge seemed to be considering things closely. Finally he shrugged. "Your word is good with me, Raine," he said with a sudden change of attitude. "Evans was evidently trying a little private grudge of his own. It didn't work. That was hard luck. Take him away, some of you men."

Cole Bridger again laughed softly. "I'm shore glad it was a private grudge of his own that he was tryin' to satisfy. I'd shore hate to think that it might have been somebody else's grudge."

Jay Partridge's swarthy face turned gray with suppressed fury. He pushed up to Cole until their eyes were not a foot apart. "You'll be wise to mind your tongue," he rasped thickly. "You're making dangerous talk that you can't back up."

"Oh, cain't I?" grinned Cole. "Try me, amigo—try me. I say what I think, regardless. An' I'm ready to back up what I say with money, marbles or chalk—or hot lead—if that'll suit yuh better. Don't bark at me, yuh half-caste crook, or I'll twist yore nose for yuh."

Something snapped in Partridge, something that held the last inch of self-control. His livid features twisted into a mask of wild hate and, with a hissing curse, his right hand darted across his body toward his left armpit.

As he started to withdraw it Cole's knees dropped together, his left shoulder sagged forward and down, and his right fist lashed out with a lifting surge of his whole body. The impact of the blow was terrific.

Jay Partridge's head snapped back, his feet left the ground and he toppled over into the crowd behind him. This unstable support gave way with oaths of astonishment, and Partridge, with all his fine panoply of raiment, rolled in the trampled dust of the street, unconscious and bleeding.

Cole straightened up coolly, blew upon his skinned knuckles, then turned to Bill Raine, who was open-mouthed with astonishment and admiration. "Sayin' which," drawled Cole, "we might as well amble along home, Mr. Raine. C'mon."

The awed crowd gave way respectfully. As Cole sauntered back to the horses, he was whistling softly between his teeth. Bill Raine, his expression almost ludicrous, plodded along at Cole's elbow. Norma, white of face, was waiting for them. She said no word as the three of them gained their saddles and spurred out of town, but she watched Cole Bridger continually, with wide, strange eyes.

Cole turned suddenly in his saddle and smiled at her. "Shore, I'm sorry yuh had to see that, Miss Raine," he drawled. "It wasn't no way pleasant for a lady's eyes."

Norma made an impatient gesture. "Don't apologize to me," she answered quickly. "I'm a woman, and I hate bloodshed and fighting. But I'm of the West, Cole

Bridger, and I know there are times when such acts are necessary. This was one of them. I'm frank to admit that I approve highly of your method of doing things."

Cole grinned boyishly. "For that I'd punch a whole flock of crooks on the nose."

Bill Raine cleared his throat harshly. "Of course yuh understand how I'm thankin' yuh, Bridger," he said. "If it wasn't for you, Norma would be an orphan right now. As it was I felt the lead stir my hair as it went by. Yeah, yuh're welcome to my friendship an' every cent of money I got. That goes."

Cole's expression turned serious and embarrassed. "Shucks, that's plumb all right, Mr. Raine. If it's won me the friendship of you an' Miss Norma, I'm plumb happy. Now let's talk of somethin' else. Yuh'll have me blushin' like a bride, first thing yuh know."

II

THE FISHHOOK RANCH LAY SOME SEVEN MILES SOUTH-west of the town of Baird. A low, arid stretch of broken ridges, called Punchbowl Hills, running roughly from northwest to southeast, separated it from Bill Raine's Half Diamond R spread.

The trails to the two ranches forked just at the base of the hills. When Cole Bridger, Norma Raine and her father reached these forks, Cole shook hands with Raine, smiled and tipped his hat to Norma and entered the malpais.

"Don't forget to come and visit us," called Norma after him.

Cole smiled again and waved reassuringly. "Yuh can bet on that," he answered. "See yuh tonight, Mr. Raine."

As he jogged his leisurely and solitary way home, Cole's brow furrowed with troubled thought. There was a problem on his mind that had been irking him for some time. Finally he shrugged. "I may be all wrong," he muttered, "but I'm gonna play safe.

"It's gonna look bad to some folks if I refuse to join up with that protective association Bill Raine is fig-gerin' on, but I ain't so shore it'd be the wise thing to do after all. There's certain folks around here I want to be a doggoned sight more shore of before I tie up with 'em. I know ole Bill is honest an' I know he means well. But some of the others—nope, they don't look good to me."

Cole's thoughts switched to Norma Raine and his brow immediately cleared. "Right interestin' appearin' young lady," he opined to himself. "Good-lookin' an' with what seems a lot of good old common sense. I shore reckon I'll accept that invitation."

Characteristically, Cole gave little thought to the shooting affair and subsequent clash with Jay Par-tridge. Cole's past life had not been lived in the shelter of peace and quiet. It had, on the contrary, been one of hard work, plenty of danger and amid surroundings which built up their own creed of ideals and decision.

Straight thoughts, straight words and straight

shooting, both literally and figuratively, summed up Cole's philosophy of life. A cowardly dry-gulcher was one to be exterminated like a treacherous snake. A four-flusher was to be called, unceremoniously. Cole had performed both duties quickly and effectively. He wasted no regrets nor suffered any apprehension over either.

As he jogged up to the ranch buildings of the Fishhook outfit, a feeling of justifiable pride swayed him. By his own hard work, frugality and self-denial, he had amassed sufficient funds to buy up this outfit, at an age when most young fellows were still engaged in having their whirl at life.

True, the place had been sadly run down when he had paid his money and taken over the deed of ownership from old Biff Williams. But Cole had been quick to add the right kind of riders to his outfit and his own enthusiasm and industry had a catching quality that soon communicated itself to his men. In three months he had made a new place out of the Fishhook Ranch.

The ranch house, set beneath the comfortable shade of a grove of cottonwoods, had been thoroughly renovated and repainted. A new bunkhouse had been built, corrals and feed sheds repaired and whitewashed. The place had taken on a look of new life and prosperity that had been lacking during the last ten years.

The range controlled by the Fishhook outfit was good range, extensive and well watered. The old mixed herd of cattle that had been taken over in the sale, Cole quickly disposed of. He brought in in their place a smaller but infinitely more profitable herd of Herefords, heavy beef cattle of the highest marketing quality and just as hardy and reproductive as the displaced stock.

During his long, lean years of saving, Cole had thought a great deal, looked and listened a lot. As a result he knew the cattle raising game better than many men twice his age.

As Cole reined in and dismounted before the corrals, two punchers came out of the bunkhouse and crossed over to him. One was lank, long-faced, and crowned with a flaming thatch of red hair. The other was short, lithe and dark of skin and hair, obviously a Mexican.

"Hello, boys," greeted Cole. "What did yore little pasear do towards clearin' up our troubles?"

Red Kester grinned, exposing a mouthful of big, white teeth. "We found that yuh were guessin' plumb correct, Cole. Mig here, worked out the trail. It was pretty badly mixed up, but there was one critter that had a split hoof an' Mig stayed with that sign like a terrier after a rat.

"The trail went across Mustard Flats an' on to the H Bar O Connected range. We lost it there, where that dry lake runs along the north edge of Mustard Flats. The hardpan comes right up to the surface in the dry lake an' of course the sign petered out on it."

"But yuh're certain the stock crossed Mustard Flats though," insisted Cole. "How about it, Mig?"

Miguel Almada's dark face broke into a sunny smile. "Quite sure, Señor Cole. I was very careful, so there

25

would be no meestake. *Sí,* they crossed Mustard Flats."

"Good work," acknowledged Cole, his eyes narrowing, lines of grimness stiffening his jaw. "I'm beginnin' to understand more every day why Biff Williams was goin' broke on a range that'll make money for 'most anybody. I'll make damn good and shore I don't travel the same trail.

"Yeah, good work, boys. Keep what yuh know absolutely to yoreselves. We'll just sling rope an' more rope until that particular jasper hangs himself plumb complete. Where's the other boys, Red?"

"I sent Foxy an' Sad over to the Cross-in-a-Box to get them bang-tails yuh bought," said Red. "Oofty is in the cook shack buildin' a mess of pies for supper. How was things in town, an' how'd the election come out?"

"Raine was beaten by fourteen votes," replied Cole. "If we'd all gone in an' voted it would have helped out some, but not enough. However, I think it's a good thing it happened as it did. It'll serve to bring matters to a haid a little quicker. It was bound to show anyhow. This neck of the woods has got a lot of poison in its system an' the sooner it gets rid of it the better off it'll be."

"Think yuh're right at that," agreed Red. "I'll bet Partridge is all swelled up on himself."

Cole smiled thinly. "Not as much as he was." And he proceeded to detail the attempt to assassinate Bill Raine, with the subsequent finish of the affair.

Miguel Almada looked grave. "That ees good and eet

26

ees bad, Señor Cole," he observed. "Een the future you must watch always over your shoulder. I know well the Evans boys. Claude was bad, but Mogy—he ees very much worse. He ees fast, veree fast weeth a gun and he weel be looking to revenge Claude. Yes, eet weel be well that you travel carefully and watch always, señor."

"Thanks for the hint, Mig," grinned Cole. "I'll do that, but I reckon this Mogy Evans will have his hands full when the time comes. As for Partridge, I wanted to let him know just where him an' me stand. An' what I mean—I got a lot of satisfaction outa that punch.

"It'll hurt him two ways. He'll get over the effects of the punch, but he suffered a let-down in dignity that ain't gonna do him a bit of good with the kind of crowd he keeps around him."

"Doggone it," mourned Red. "Yuh did somethin', boss, that I been yearnin' to do for a long time. If I could get just one good ole roundhouse smack at Partridge I'd feel that life was plumb complete."

Cole chuckled. "Unless I'm way off in my figgerin', Red, yuh'll have plenty of chance to rectify yore wasted, misspent life. There's clouds gatherin' over this range, dark clouds that'll take a lot of gunpowder an' hot lead to blast away. I'm bettin' even you'll get yore fill of trouble, yuh sorrel-topped ape."

The assemblage in Ezra Hoskins' big storeroom was complete by eight o'clock. There were eight men present in the actual room. Outside, perched on the edge of the splintery boardwalk before the store, three others were squatted. While momentous conference was to be held inside, Lon Sheer, Jim Early and Red Kester lolled in the warm, seductive moonlight, smoked innumerable cigarettes and swapped awesome lies.

Inside, by common consent, Bill Raine had taken charge of the meeting. Raine had perched himself on an upturned molasses keg, while the rest found various positions among the miscellaneous piles of supplies that nearly filled the storeroom. Raine wasted no time in coming to the point.

"You men know I got a lickin' today," he began quietly. "I could have won if yuh'd been on yore toes an' backed me to the limit. However, that's neither here nor there an' I'm not cryin' about it. Yet we gotta face this fact. The wrong kind of crowd is in power. We all know what sort of a hombre Jay Partridge is; we've seen him operate. He's greedy, ambitious and crooked.

"Claude Evans tried to plug me today, plug me in the back. He'd got away with it too, if it hadn't been for Cole Bridger's quick thinkin' an' shootin'. Of course I cain't prove it, but I'm damn shore Partridge was behind the move. I'm tellin' yuh this just to show yuh what we can expect in the future.

"Partridge an' his crowd got their eyes on this whole range around here an' they mean to have it if they can get their way in things. I thought it might be a good idee for us cattlemen to get together an' form a kind of mutual protection society. If we keep on workin' alone, Partridge will be able to take us one at a time an' put the skids under us.

"If we stick together an' fight him as a unit we can pick his tail-feathers plumb complete. If we don't— well, the answer is plain. Get me right; this ain't sour grapes I'm advocatin'. It's plumb common sense as I see it. Now this is open meetin' an' I want everybody to give their idees on the subject. . . . Pat, what d'yuh think of it?"

Pat Ryan, a thin, monkey-looking little fellow, spat emphatically. "Yore talk listens good to me, Bill," he rasped nasally. "Just consider the Cross-in-a-Box at yore disposal any time. I see yore point an' I'm for it."

To this Jack Batten, Tim Harding and Frenchy Gaston nodded agreement. "We're with yuh, Bill," they conceded.

Raine nodded happily, glad to see that his idea was taking such substantial form. He turned to another member of the assemblage. "How about you, Hack?"

Hack Orcutt shifted restlessly. He was a big man, heavy of shoulder and neck, with a square face, tight of mouth and narrow of eye. "Well, yes and no, Bill," he growled cautiously. "I'm frank to admit that I think yuh're kinda overdrawin' the danger quite a bit. I agree that Jay Partridge is not the kind of sheriff we want.

"It's too bad all us fellers was so over-confident that we let him steer the election like he did. But I reckon yuh've overdrawn his ambitions. Me, I think his main idee in gainin' office was more to make shore that his little graft here in town wasn't disturbed."

Pat Ryan snorted. "That's foolish," he stated bluntly. "Did Bill ever interfere with Partridge as long as he kept his joint reasonably decent an' ran his games halfway square? No, he never did. Bill's right on this, Hack.

"Partridge has got his gun loaded for big game. We're it. Get on the bandwagon with the rest of us an' quit bein' so gol-blasted stubborn. If yuh'd thought of the scheme first yuh'd been yelpin' for it like a lonesome maverick."

Orcutt scowled at the fiery little Irishman. "I don't need you to make up my mind for me, Pat. I still think Bill's overdrawin' things."

"Aw, hell," broke in Jack Batten. "Yuh don't stand to lose nothin' by it, Hack. It's just a safety first idee. If we never need to call on each other for help, why that'll suit all of us fine. But if we ever do, a little outside help will come in mighty handy. It won't cost yuh nothin', if that's what's worryin' yuh."

This remark brought out several chuckles, as Hack Orcutt's penny-pinching propensities were well known by the others. Orcutt's heavy face turned angry red. "Lemme ask yuh somethin'," he growled. "Is he comin' in on this thing, too?"

Hack Orcutt nodded towards Cole Bridger, who had been a silent and secretly amused spectator up until now.

Bill Raine's head jerked up at the question. "Shore he is," he rumbled half angrily. "Why not?"

"That's it," chimed in Pat Ryan. "Why not? He's a cattle rancher, same as the rest of us an' one of the crowd."

Orcutt shook his head heavily. "Then yuh can count me out. The rest of us here are ole-timers in these parts. Bridger's a newcomer. He ain't proved himself yet, no more than Jay Partridge has for that matter. This association has gotta be air-tight, or I'm havin' nothin' to do with it."

Bill Raine jumped to his feet. "Just what in hell do yuh mean by that kinda talk, Orcutt?" he began belligerently. "Me, I'm resentin' such remarks agin a friend of—"

"Just a minute, Mr. Raine," broke in Cole drawlingly. "I'm thankin' yuh for them words an' the spirit that prompts 'em, but I can see Orcutt's point. I am a newcomer here an' mebbe I see things different than the rest of yuh. Bein' new, mebbe I see things most of yuh don't see at all.

"Now I wouldn't for the world break up yore association. You ole-timers go ahead an' make up yore combine. I'll shuffle along alone for a time. Mebbe later, Orcutt might change his mind. If he does, I'll be most happy to sit in with the rest of yuh.

"No," he went on quickly, as he saw that Bill Raine was thoroughly wrathy at Orcutt and sputtering to get his heated words out; "don't get to quarrelin' over me. I can paddle my own boat. An' though I'm not a real member of yore combine—just remember this, all of yuh: Any time yuh might need help, yuh know where

31

to come to get it. An' now, gentlemen—good night an' good luck."

Cole had been on his feet while he was talking, and now he moved to the door. As he finished his words, he slipped through the doorway and was gone.

Bill Raine foamed like an over-wrought grizzly. "Dammit! I got a good notion to belt yuh over yore thick, stubborn haid with a whiffle tree, Hack Orcutt. That boy is a friend of mine—a darn good friend. He saved my life today. He means more to me than you ever did.

"If it wasn't that I'd called you fellers all the way in from yore spreads tonight, an' if I didn't feel that it's necessary for us to get together, damned if I wouldn't pick up an' get out myself. Of all the pig-haided, selfish, dumb, stupid—"

"Sentiments seconded and approved, Bill," broke in Pat Ryan. "That boy Bridger is clean stuff. Any man with half an eye can see it. . . . Hack, what the devil yuh got against the kid, anyhow?"

"Yuh heard what I said," snapped Orcutt angrily. "All I say is wait a couple of years from now. If Bridger is still comin' along in good shape I won't kick a bit then at lettin' him in with us. I just don't believe in goin' off half cocked, that's all."

Frenchy Gaston spoke up. Gaston was a big fellow, of French-Canadian extraction, quiet and grave. "Me, I think Hack is wrong myself. But Bridger won't lack for help, even if he ain't one of this association we're talkin' of. Me an' my men will be ready to ride for him any time. Now let's get down to business an' get this thing settled. Squabblin' ain't gonna get us nowhere."

There was wisdom in Frenchy's words, so the Rhyolite Cattlemen's Association was formed, with Hack Orcutt, still seemingly reluctant, finally agreeing to membership. When the meeting broke up and Bill Raine went out he found only the faithful Lon Sheer and Jim Early waiting for him. Cole Bridger and Red Kester had gone.

"They left a good hour ago," answered Early to Raine's question.

Raine muttered a curse and swung into his saddle, leading the way out towards his ranch. Hack Orcutt and Tim Harding rode off together as their ranches lay northwest of town, while Jack Batten, Pat Ryan and Frenchy Gaston formed another group, riding east.

By the time the meeting broke up, Cole Bridger and Red Kester were far from town, riding northwest. They traveled swiftly, saying nothing, heading directly for the H Bar O Connected range. When they had rounded the northern end of the Punchbowl Hills, they cut across between the H Bar O Connected ranch buildings and Mustard Flats.

"They keep their Hereford herd over west, don't they?" asked Cole at length.

Red Kester nodded. "Yeah. That's their best range an' "—here Red smiled thinly—"it's handiest to the railroad. Their longhorn an' poorer grade stuff they run along the north end of Punchbowl Hills an' around

Mustard Flats. But I don't see yet, boss, how yuh expect to locate anythin' in the dark thisaway. One whiteface looks a lot like another at any time an' it's too cussed black to read a brand."

"Hum," grunted Cole. "Mebbe so. But if yuh remember, one of that herd you an' Mig was trailin' was that ole cow that got nearly hamstrung by them two lobo wolves we been havin' trouble with. The critter had a kind of hitchety, jumpity walk. If we stir around we may locate it."

For the past mile or so they had been coming upon small groups of resting cattle, cattle which snorted and moved aside as they passed. The clacking of horns soon told Cole that these were longhorns, and he wasn't interested.

Finally a dark line of massed willows and taller cottonwood trees took form before them. The moist, heavy smell of water was in the air. "Here's Cottonwood Creek," said Cole. "An' there's Shirt-Tail Bend over to the left. We'll look around in that meadow inside the bend."

They splashed across the creek, pausing long enough for their horses to gulp a little water. They came out into a wide, verdant meadow, lying inside a big bend in the creek, which came down from the north, swung west and then turned northwest. Here they immediately came upon Hereford cattle, their snowy faces and throats looming in pale patches through the darkness.

"We split up here an' circulate, Red," ordered Cole. "Stir every whiteface yuh see into action an' watch for one that limps some. When yuh locate that one, rope an' throw it an' take a look at the brand."

Red swung down along the course of the creek, while Cole cut straight out into the meadow, riding slowly and urging the cattle he came upon in movement, taking care that he did not frighten them into stampede.

It looked like a hopeless task. There were hundreds of cattle in the big meadow, attracted by the verdant pasture and the presence of nearby water. A few longhorns wandered about, animals that had strayed from the range farther east.

Time passed—an hour, then another. Red and Cole met at the far edge of the meadow and compared notes. "The most sound-laiged bunch of critters I ever run across," asseverated Red. "Not a cripple in the layout that I could see. Mebbe they did away with that old cow, boss, figgerin' that it could be identified."

"Maybe they did," agreed Cole. "Looks like we had our ride for nothin', Red. Well, we might as well be gettin' home. C'mon."

Cole reined about and headed for the creek again. He was disappointed, having gambled a great deal on this little sortie. Had the presence of Red and himself been discovered by any of the H Bar O Connected riders, awkward explanations would have had to be made. It was not considered exactly ethical for riders to be browsing about among the herds of another ranch during the dark of night.

As they emerged on the east side of the creek they

heard the rustle of movement off to their right. Cole's eyes darted keenly about. He located a Hereford moving slowly away. And the animal had a distinct, dragging limp!

"Keno!" he exclaimed swiftly. "Here's what we're lookin' for, Red. C'mon. I'll chuck a rope on it an' we'll look it over. Hey! What the devil—"

"What's wrong?" demanded Red alertly.

"Well, shore that's funny," drawled Cole. "I'd 'a' sworn I had my riata along—yuh know, Red, that horsehair one that Mig made for me. Anyway, it's gone now. Here, lemme yores."

Red handed over his braided rawhide lariat and Cole, spurring up beside the limping Hereford, dropped a loop over the animal's stubby horns. Then he flipped the rope over and down in a dragging line beyond the animal's rear feet. Whirling his bronc to one side, he cut the Hereford's legs neatly from under it, dropping it with a thud.

Leaving the intelligent horse to keep the rope singing tight, Cole dismounted and went up to the struggling cow, Red following him. While Red knelt on the brute's neck Cole snapped a match alight and looked over the brand on the Hereford's flank. He bent lower, running a forefinger along the lines of the brand. Presently he straightened up and blew out the match.

"Okeh," he said coldly. "Just as we thought, Red. Somebody has run a H Bar O Connected over my Fishhook iron, an' they did a kind of botchy job at that. The barefaced nerve of 'em! Well, let the brute go. I told yuh if we gave enough rope a certain jasper would be hangin' himself. He ain't far from the noose right now."

Red slipped the riata from the Hereford's horns and he and Cole went back to their horses. As they rode away, Red coiled his rope and strapped it to his saddle. "No wonder Williams went broke on the Fishhook spread, boss," he murmured. "Pore, dumb ole devil went broke an' couldn't figger why. We could tell him, all right."

Cole nodded, saying nothing. But his eyes were chill and narrow and his face set in grim determination. On the morrow, certain folks would have a lot to explain. Despite the importance of what he had just discovered, Cole found time to puzzle at the disappearance of his riata, the horsehair one Mig Almada had labored so lovingly over, and then, in a gesture of respect and affection, had presented to his boss.

Cole prized the rope highly, for the thought that had come with it as well as for its beautiful workmanship. He had been positive that it was strapped in its accustomed place against the pommel of his saddle when he had ridden into Baird earlier that evening.

Evidently, while he had been in Ezra Hoskins' store with the others, some wandering and unscrupulous individual had glimpsed the rope and appropriated it. Cole had the satisfaction of knowing that whoever stole it would have a hard time using it unless he rode completely out of the country, for the lariat was pretty well known and would be easily recognized.

Cole's thoughts went back to the meeting at Hoskins' store. He smiled a tight, grim smile. He was understanding more and more all the time. There were white men, here about the Punchbowl Hills range, but there were off-color ones also. He was glad that he had not joined the association. Being a free agent, bound by no rulings of any sort, would prove a distinct advantage now.

When Cole and Red rode up to the Fishhook Ranch they found everything in darkness and quiet. They put their mounts in the corrals; Red went to the bunkhouse and Cole up to the big house. Ten minutes later they were both asleep.

Cole awoke abruptly, conscious of the presence of several people in his room. It was gray dawn and the air was chill. He raised himself on one elbow and stared straight into the muzzle of a flat, snub-nosed, wicked-looking automatic. The automatic was held by none other than Jay Partridge, newly elected sheriff of Rhyolite County.

In back of Partridge stood Bill Raine, Jim Early, Lon Sheer and Hack Orcutt. Orcutt looked somewhat disheveled and pale. There was a bulge under Orcutt's right pants leg, about halfway up the thigh. As he moved slightly to one side, Cole saw that Orcutt limped.

Mastering his surprise, Cole looked over his visitors calmly. "Well, gents—why the artillery and serious looks? Raine, you an' yore two men seem to be keeping bad company."

Bill Raine winced under the sarcasm of Cole's words. "Yuh got me wrong, lad," he explained hastily. "Me an' the boys are here to see that yuh get a square deal, that's all. We don't believe yuh did it."

"Hum," grunted Cole, thinking swiftly. "I don't know what yuh're drivin' at, but I'm apologizin' to yuh. I shoulda knowed better than to link yuh with polecats."

Jay Partridge's face, bruised and puffed from the blow Cole had dealt him the previous day in Baird, twisted into a malignant leer of triumph. "You're under arrest, Bridger," he snapped. "And anything you say will be used against you."

"Yuh don't say so," drawled Cole. "If I may ask, what am I under arrest for?"

"The murder of Tim Harding."

Cole sat up slowly, indubitable surprise showing in his widened eyes. "The murder of Tim Harding? Why, yuh're crazy! I ain't seen Harding since I left Hoskins' store last night. Why in hell should I murder Tim Harding? He seemed like a mighty nice sort to me an' I liked him. When did all this happen?"

Partridge did not answer. Instead he asked another question. "Where were you last night after you left Hoskins' store? Did you come straight home?"

As Cole studied Partridge's expression he knew that the latter had deliberately baited a trap for him. Partridge's eyes were a little too eager. Cole shook his head. "No, I didn't. Red Kester an' me took a little ride—on private business."

Bill Raine lifted a quick hand in protest. "Go slow, Cole—go slow on what yuh say. Better wait an' say nothin' until yore lawyer arrives. I sent word to Freeburg for one already. Wait until he gets here an' let him do yore talkin' for yuh."

"Shore that's decent of yuh, Mr. Raine," replied Cole. "But ain't yuh jaspers tryin' to pull some joke or somethin'? I ain't done nothin' to need a lawyer for. I tell yuh I never saw Tim Harding after I left the store. He was still there an' in good health when I left. Yuh cain't pin any killin' on me. Just who besides you, Partridge, is accusin' me of killin' Tim?"

"You'll find that out soon enough, Bridger. Get your clothes on. I'm takin' you to jail. And remember, if you make a phony move I'll plug you. I'm the duly elected sheriff of this county and if you fight back you're fightin' the law."

"He's right, Cole," broke in Bill Raine. "Go along with him peaceable. He'd like nothing better than an excuse to rock yuh off under the pretense that yuh were resistin' arrest."

Partridge tossed a malignant look over his shoulder at Raine. "The quicker you learn to mind your own business from here on out the better it will be for you, Raine," he snarled.

Tall, lean, still-faced Jim Early moved slightly. "The boss an' Lon an' me are makin' this affair our business all the way through," said the Texan softly. "Yuh wanta get used to us, Mister Sheriff, 'cause we shore aim to stick around."

Partridge's dark face flushed lividly and he angrily chewed at his lip. But he did not answer Early. He turned back to Cole, who was slowly drawing on his trousers and boots. Cole was looking at Hack Orcutt.

"What yuh limpin' about, Orcutt?" asked Cole casually.

Orcutt's heavy face twisted. "Yuh know damn well why I'm limpin'," he growled. "Yuh tried to plug me as well as Tim. The best yuh could do was jam a slug through my laig."

Cole grinned in bewilderment. "Well, may I be bit by a horned toad! Ain't wonders ever gonna cease? They tell me I shot pore Tim Harding an' that I winged the estimable Mister Orcutt. Pretty soon they'll be sayin' I put salt in King George's tea. You fellers grow funnier all the time."

"Mebbe yuh won't think things so funny when they knot a rope around yore neck, feller," retorted Orcutt. He moved again to ease his leg and Cole saw that Orcutt held something in his hand. Cole's eyes narrowed.

"Speakin' of ropes," he drawled, "where did yuh get that horsehair riata yuh're packin', Orcutt?"

Orcutt grinned maliciously. "Where d'yuh suppose? We found it strung in the brush right alongside the trail where yuh shot Tim Harding an' me. When yuh were makin' yore getaway it musta caught on the brush an' jerked loose from yore saddle. Try an' laugh that off!"

41

III

W<small>HEN</small> B<small>ILL</small> R<small>AINE</small> <small>RODE SLOWLY HOME AT TEN</small> o'clock that morning, he found Norma waiting on the wide veranda of the Half Diamond R ranch house. The moment he dismounted she came over to him.

"Dad," she demanded, "what's the matter? What has happened? Who was it that came here early this morning and got you out of bed? I woke up at the noise, but you left so quickly I didn't have time to find out what it was all about."

Raine put his arm about her as he plodded wearily up onto the porch and sank into a comfortable, rawhide-backed chair. "The snakes are beginnin' to crawl, the coyotes are howlin' an' the human buzzards are gatherin' for the feast, honey," he said slowly. "They've got Cole Bridger an' Red Kester in jail, charged with killin' Tim Harding an' woundin' Hack Orcutt."

The color in Norma's face receded slightly. "No!" she answered vehemently. "Why, that's impossible!"

"Shore it's impossible," nodded Raine wearily. "The killin' part, I mean. Cole an' Red ain't the kind to shoot a man in the back. But they're in jail, just the same. That noise yuh heard this mornin' was Hack Orcutt comin' after me. He had a bullet hole through his laig which we had to tie up.

"Then we left for town. Hack was insistent on gettin'

42

Jay Partridge. We rode on to where the shootin' happened an' Partridge looked things over. There was pore ole Tim Harding, shore enough—an' shot in the back."

"But how did Orcutt figure in things, Dad?" asked Norma.

"Him an' Tim rode off together after the meetin' last night. The same trail leads to their ranches, yuh know. Accordin' to Orcutt's story, they was amblin' along slow and easy. Just as they was circlin' the north end of Punchbowl Hills range, somebody opened up on 'em from the brush beside the trail. Tim got it cold, the very first shot. Orcutt drags his gun an' whirls, tryin' to fight back.

"As he does so he takes one through the laig. His hoss is scared and startin' to pitch some. Orcutt couldn't grip the saddle with his crippled laig an' got throwed. Evidently the dry-gulchers figgered that they'd downed both men, for they lit out, hellity-larrup. Orcutt was pretty badly shaken up an' lost some blood. He's quite a while gettin' so he can hobble around.

"He manages to ketch his hoss an' he rode straight out here, 'cause we formed our protective association last night, an' I'm the chairman of it. He wanted to find out what I thought we should do. I told him I was willin' to give Partridge a chance to act, providin' he got results. If he didn't we'd take up matters in the association. So we got Partridge an' rode on out like I told you."

"But what made Partridge think that Cole—Mr.

Bridger—and Red Kester had anything to do with it?" asked Norma.

"I was gettin' to that," rumbled Raine. "Partridge begins prowlin' around in the brush, lookin' for tracks. An' what does he find but Cole Bridger's horsehair riata that Mig Almada made an' gave to Cole. It's strung out through the brush, like it had been caught an' jerked off the saddle.

"Everybody knows that riata. Partridge didn't wait for anythin' more. He hates Bridger like poison, after the way Bridger knocked him down yesterday an' made a fool of him in front of all his friends. Well, we roused Cole outa bed an' Partridge arrested him for murder—him an' Red Kester."

"But the lariat doesn't prove anything," argued Norma stubbornly. "Someone might have planted it there, figuring they'd get Mr. Bridger in trouble."

"My own thought," nodded Raine. "But when Partridge asked Cole where he went after leavin' the meetin'—Orcutt objected to Cole's membership yuh know, an' Cole left ahaid of the rest of us—Cole told him it was none of his affair. Said he an' Red took a little ride on private business.

"That was playin' right into Partridge's hands. I tried to get Cole to stop talkin', but he was mad an' reckless an' wouldn't keep still. I know Cole ain't guilty—he just ain't the sort to pull a thing like that—but things look mighty bad for him."

Norma was twisting her hands unconsciously, her eyes shadowed with worry. "The whole thing is ridiculous," she quavered. "Charging Mr. Bridger with murder, I mean. Why, he had no motive, did he? Has he ever fought with Tim Harding?"

Raine shook his head. "Not that I know of. Cole seemed real upset to hear that Tim was daid. Claimed he liked Tim a lot. I don't know why I feel like I do, but somethin' tells me the whole thing is a frame-up."

"We've got to get a lawyer—a good one, right away," decided Norma, her eyes flashing.

Raine smiled faintly. "I've already sent for one, honey. Oh, I'm gonna see that Cole an' Red get a fair break. I can see that Partridge don't like the way I'm stickin' by Cole. Hack Orcutt told me I was a fool for doin' it, but I like Cole an' he looks like clean stuff to me.

"I've left Jim Early an' Lon Sheer in town, with orders to stay there an' keep an' eye on things. I wouldn't put it beyond Partridge to try an' frame a lynchin' bee."

"I'm glad you did that, Dad," said Norma swiftly. "Any mob will think twice before they try and face Lon and Jim. Didn't Partridge question Hack Orcutt's story? Personally, I wouldn't trust Orcutt very far. He's got a treacherous look about him somehow."

Raine shook his head. "Orcutt gathered in a slug himself, yuh want to remember. Tim didn't fire a shot. We looked at his gun. Every chamber was loaded an' the barrel was clean an' full of oil. No, I reckon Hack's story is straight enough. He'd got no cause to shoot Tim. Him an' Tim were neighbors an' good friends as far as I know. It's a frame-up against Cole, an' I'll bet a laig Partridge is behind it. Well, reckon I'll get some breakfast. I'm half starved."

Norma knitted her smooth brow in thought. "I'm going in and see Mr. Bridger," she determined suddenly. "After what he did for you and me yesterday, Dad, I want him to know that we're backing him to the limit. Do you think Partridge will let me see him?"

"He cain't well refuse yuh, honey. Especially if Lon an' Jim go along when yuh make yore request. Fly to it, an' see that Cole an' Red have some decent food served 'em. I'll be in town later on, to meet the stage from Freeburg. That lawyer I was tellin' yuh about oughta be on it."

While her father headed kitchenward, Norma sped to her room where she changed swiftly to riding togs. She wondered vaguely at her own interest and vehement partisanship in the affair. She felt as though an old and very dear friend was in danger. Though her actual acquaintance with Cole Bridger was hardly twenty-four hours old, she felt as though she had known him for years.

And then there was something else, some inner tumult that had stirred, deep within the depths of her, that made her pink of cheek and bright of eye. The brightness of a dauntless spirit girding itself for combat—combat to be fought for an ideal, or for a slumberous, deep and newfound emotion.

At the corrals Norma expertly roped and saddled a speedy bronc, flung herself into the saddle and spurred away at a fast run. She realized perfectly that there was no need of such haste, yet something was urging her on, some dominant desire to see Cole Bridger and to assure him of the faith and unbending support of her father and herself.

It was as though she was seeking vindication in Cole Bridger's eyes—an establishment of regard and trust. Just why she felt so she could not define, but the feeling persisted and whipped her on, just the same.

There was a subdued air of excitement about the town of Baird when Norma Raine pounded into it, to draw her bronc to a rearing halt before the sheriff's office and jail. She dismounted and tethered the sweating, panting horse, then looked around.

With a thrill of satisfaction she saw two tall, easily moving punchers evolve out of the doorway of Hoskins' store and come sauntering towards her. Those two were Lon Sheer and Jim Early.

These silent, grave men were somewhat of enigmas to Norma. They had ridden up to her father's ranch one day some four years before and had been put to work immediately. They had remained ever since, still, efficient, trustful punchers. They were inseparable pals. Wherever one was seen the other was sure to be somewhere close at hand.

Of their past lives, Norma knew little. She had heard it rumored once that they had served together in the Texas Rangers, but had left, due to some difference of opinion with a political faction that was trying to get control of that famous Border patrol. Certainly Lon and Jim never talked of their past.

Norma had never heard of either of them ever having thrown a gun since coming to the Half Diamond R Ranch, yet when they spoke up where conflict of some kind hovered, men listened and quieted. There was a suggestion of terrible, potent power about them that was undefinable but ever present. Secretly, Norma was just a little afraid of them, like a small child might be of some figment of imagination.

In their personal treatment of Norma they had been ever kind, courteous, and gravely obliging. Their gaze was always respectful, and at times, almost wistfully gentle. They were men of steel and sinew, forged and molded in adversity and danger, harshened by rough contact, yet retaining a kindness and purity of eye that set them apart and strangely ennobled them.

"Lon—Jim," cried Norma, as they came up. "I was hoping I'd see you."

"Nothin' wrong out at the ranch, is there, Miss Norma?" drawled Early.

"Nothing. But I want to have a chance to talk with Cole Bridger and I don't know whether Partridge will allow me to see him. Dad suggested that if you and Lon came with me when I made my request of the sheriff, he probably would grant it."

"I shouldn't wonder but what yore daddy was right," nodded Early gravely. "Suppose we see Partridge an' have a powwow with him? He's in the office. I saw him go in about ten minutes ago."

Early stepped up to the door and knocked. The door

opened and Jay Partridge stood there. He scowled as he saw Lon and Jim, but the scowl faded to an oily, ingratiating smile when his eyes met Norma's fresh, eager young face. He bowed slightly.

"Ah—good morning, Miss Raine. Did you wish to see me about something?"

"Yes," replied Norma shortly, making no attempt to hide her dislike for the newly elected sheriff. "I wish to see Mr. Bridger and have a little talk with him."

The smile left Partridge's face. His eyes glinted warily. He shook his head. "I'm afraid that is impossible," he answered glibly. "I'm really sorry. But Bridger is a murderer and a desperate man. I don't feel that I can afford to take any chance, however slight, of giving him a chance to escape."

"Bosh!" exclaimed Norma spiritedly. "Mr. Bridger is neither a murderer nor a desperate man. And I fail to understand just what you mean by your last remark. Are you hinting that I might help him to get away?"

"I was sorta wonderin' that myself," broke in Lon Sheer gravely. "Yuh wasn't by any chance meanin' such a thing, was yuh, Partridge?"

Lon's voice was soft, almost gentle, but there was an intentness in his chill, unwinking look that caused Partridge to flush and shift his eyes.

"Of course not—of course not," said the sheriff hastily. "I only meant that the fewer visitors Bridger has, the less likelihood there would be of any slight chance by which he might profit in a break for liberty. That was all."

"Um," nodded Lon. "Well, in this case, there won't be no chance, so I reckon Miss Norma can see him. Don't yuh think?"

Another look at Lon's face decided Partridge that Norma *could* see Cole, so he stepped aside and motioned them to enter. A hard, bitter, ugliness had formed about his mouth, however, and as Lon and Jim entered behind Norma, the glitter in Partridge's black eyes was venomous. Selecting two chairs, the Texans sat down, lounging lazily.

"Take all the time yuh want, Miss Norma," drawled Early. "These chairs are plumb comfortable an' it's nice an' cool in here. Don't hurry none on our account."

With a show of bustling authority, Partridge went to the rear of his office and unlocked a heavy door. Beyond this was a dark, short hall with another heavy door at the far end, also locked.

"This way, Miss Raine," he said curtly.

Norma followed him into the hall and he swung the first door to and locked it. Then he unlocked the second door, which led into the jail. The jail was a small, single-roomed building, containing several bunks and lit by half a dozen windows less than a foot square and heavily barred.

"A visitor to see you, Bridger," announced Partridge.

As Norma stepped into the jail, the door behind her clanged shut and the lock clicked. She heard Partridge's footsteps echo as he went back to his office. For a moment she had the queer feeling of being in a trap. She immediately conquered this, however, remembering that Lon and Jim were out there with Partridge.

When Cole Bridger realized who his visitor was, he rose from where he had been lounging on a bunk, and came forward with unbelieving eagerness shining in his eyes.

"Miss Raine—Norma!" Cole exclaimed. "What brings yuh here?"

Norma was suddenly timid, self-conscious. The light in Cole Bridger's eyes at once thrilled and frightened her. She saw Red Kester also rolling off a bunk and climbing to his feet.

"I—I just had to see you," she stammered, searching frantically for words. "You see, I—Dad—well, we wanted you to know that we do not believe for a second that you are guilty."

She realized that somehow Cole Bridger had secured possession of both her hands and was holding them gently. She knew her own were trembling, but they stilled before the warm pressure given them.

"Shore," said Cole a trifle huskily. "Shore, that's mighty fine an' kind of yuh. An' I want yuh to know that yore confidence ain't a mite misplaced. Me an' Red never had a thing to do with that killin'. Why, I valued Tim Harding as a real friend, even though I hadn't known him long. He was my style of a man."

"I know," said Norma. "You've been framed; I'm sure of it. But tell me, how did your lariat happen to be found near the scene of the murder?"

"Wish I knew," answered Cole grimly. "I missed that lariat last night, after Red an' me had left town. Somebody lifted it off my saddle an' planted it with malice plumb aforethought. Now I'm gonna tell yuh somethin', Miss Norma—somethin' I want yuh to tell yore daddy an' make him believe. Partridge ain't the only snake in the grass around these parts.

"There are others an' they're men yore dad calls his friends. Partridge thinks he's got the daid wood on Red an' me because we won't tell him where we went last night after leavin' town. We didn't go home right away. But we did go over across Cottonwood Creek an' over there we found a Hereford critter with a blotted brand. My Fishhook iron had been run into a H Bar O Connected."

The color faded from Norma's face again. "That's a pretty strong indictment against Hack Orcutt, Cole," she said, her eyes serious and troubled.

Cole shrugged. "It's the truth."

"It shore is, Miss Norma," broke in Red Kester. "Things are just exactly like the boss puts it."

"I'm not questioning it at all, Red. . . . And Cole, you want me to tell Dad that?"

"Tell him to keep it under his hat," cautioned Cole hastily. "An' yuh might get word to the boys at my spread not to do anythin' rash. They're all boiled up about me an' Red bein' in the calaboose an' liable to go off at a tangent any time. Yuh tell 'em my orders are to sit tight an' wait until they hear from me."

"I'll do that also, Cole," promised Norma.

Cole squeezed her hands tighter. "Yuh're a jewel," he said softly. "Yuh cain't imagine what this visit means to me, Norma."

She avoided his eyes again, because that queer, panicky feeling had gripped her once more. "Dad said I was to see that you had good food served you," she stated, changing the subject. "And he has a lawyer coming in on the afternoon stage.

"Oh, we'll see that you get a square deal. And now I must be going."

As she went up the little hall, she sensed Jay Partridge's black eyes upon her. Partridge was scowling. Then he forced a mechanical smile as he unlocked the second door and let her out into the office. Lon Sheer and Jim Early, after swift glances at Norma's face, nodded and stood up.

"Have a right nice visit, Miss Norma?" drawled Lon.

Norma colored slightly. "Yes, indeed, Lon. Thank you very much, Mr. Partridge, for the courtesy. Incidentally, I'm leaving orders at the hash-house for meals to be sent to your two prisoners. I hope that will be all right with you."

"That is quite all right with me, Miss Raine. I'll see that Bridger and Kester get their meals promptly. I see I was wrong in wishing to keep you from visiting the prisoners. In the future, unless I receive court orders to the contrary, you are welcome to visit them as often as you please."

Norma was somewhat startled by this announce-

53

ment, but she hid her surprise very well. "Thank you," she acknowledged.

When Norma and the two Texans had left the office, Partridge settled himself in the chair behind his desk and lit a long, black perfecto. His eyes grew half lidded, thoughtful, and a little red glow built up in them.

"You almost overlooked that bet, Partridge," he told himself softly. "This range is full of prizes and not the least of them is that girl. Why, she's a raving little beauty."

He was still sitting there motionless, his thoughts busy over dark speculation, when another knock sounded on his door. He straightened up, and slid his right hand beneath the left lapel of his coat.

"Come on in," he called.

The door opened and shut quickly as a lank, travel-stained, thin-faced rider slipped through. At sight of the newcomer, Jay Partridge's eyes snapped with satisfaction. "Hello, Mogy," he greeted. "Glad to see you. You got my message all right?"

The newcomer nodded, his expression stony. "Yeah," he croaked harshly, "I got it. An' I relayed yore instructions to Condon an' his crowd. They ought to drag in sometime tonight. I'm gonna be glad to see tonight get here," he finished significantly.

"I suppose you'll be right there to pull on the rope, eh Mogy?" Partridge smiled thinly.

The puncher cursed venomously. "An' then some. They tell me he shot Claude plumb through the throat."

Partridge nodded. "Yes, he did. Bridger is fast, damn him—a regular streak of lightning with a gun. Bridger shoved Raine out of line of Claude's bullet an' with almost the same move drew and shot back. I'm sorry, Mogy, but I think Claude was just a little incautious."

Mogy Evans licked his thin, tight lips. He nodded slightly. "Musta been careless, all right. With first chance like he had he oughta got 'em both—cold. Mebbe he'd been drinkin' too much."

"Perhaps. Well, you'll get your satisfaction tonight. You can handle Bridger any way you want as long as you make sure of him."

"I'll make sure—double sure. While he's kickin' on the rope I'm puttin' a gun load of lead through him. By the way, I see they're gettin' wise to Orcutt already."

Partridge lurched half out of his chair, his teeth coming together with a snap. "What? What do you mean? How do you know?"

Evans stared at Partridge in amazement. "Does it matter that much, boss?"

"Does it matter? It matters plenty," gritted Partridge. "How did you get wind of it?"

"Why I was comin' in behind the jail just now—I didn't wanta make myself too conspicuous around town for a time—I heard Bridger an' that Raine girl talkin'. I sneaked up under the window and listened. I heard Bridger tell the girl that him an' Red Kester had found a Hereford critter with a Fishhook iron blotted to a H Bar O Connected. He told her to tell her father about it."

55

Partridge came to his feet, cursing. "I might have known it—I might have known it!" he raved. "That's where him an' Kester were last night, eh? Damn that bungling Orcutt, anyhow. If all his brains were in a nutshell they'd rattle like a pea in a pod. The damned idiot! Leaving a rustled cow around where the owner could stumble on it!

"Mogy, I got somethin' for yuh to do—an' do fast. Sift out the back way, same as you came. Grab your bronc and make a wide circle, hitting the Half Diamond R trail somewhere past the forks. You've got to beat the girl to it. I think she'll be alone. When she shows up, grab her.

"Get hold of her somehow and take her out to that old sheep-herder's cabin back in the roughs on Table Mountain. Hold her until I send someone out to relieve you. I'll have them there as soon as possible. You'll have plenty of time to get back in town for the fun."

Mogy Evans got up from the chair he had taken. "I'll do it," he growled. "But I don't see what for. Yuh'll raise more hell by stealin' that girl than yuh would if yuh rustled every haid of stock within a hundred miles."

Partridge shrugged. "Can't help it now. If she gets word to her father about what Orcutt's been doing, there is no tellin' what will happen."

Mogy nodded, pulled on his hat, and slipped out. Partridge got to his feet and soon left the office.

IV

THE DOMINATION OF RHYOLITE COUNTY POLITICS, PLUS
the attendant scheme of loot and oppression, was the
most ambitious gamble Jay Partridge had ever
attempted. As far back as he could remember the virus
of chance taking had been the ruling passion in his life.
But as he grew older he soon realized that chance
taking did not bring a percentage of profit, when
played as pure chance. The odds had to be manipulated, if one was to prosper at the game.

As a gambler at the card table he had seen to it that
the odds were manipulated. Those long, smooth,
scrupulously cared for fingers of his had achieved a
dexterity with the paste boards that defied the keenest
eyes. It had been years since he had dealt an honest
game, but the mere fact that he was still alive and that
men still played with him, was a murky monument to
the flawless craft of those fingers.

Yet, as Partridge stood momentarily on the steps of
the sheriff's office and looked up and down the street,
where the sun poured down in white brilliance on the
dust, he realized that there was a vast difference in the
other games he had sat into, when compared to the present one. In the others, he alone manipulated the cards
and success or failure rested entirely on his own speed
and deftness. He had to depend on no one else, run no
chance of another's blundering.

But this was a larger game, infinitely so; much too large for one man to handle. Partridge had realized that when he first formulated the idea. To put it over he needed help, allies. Certain workings of it had to be placed in the hands of others. He had to run the risk of someone blundering and, from what Mogy Evans had just told him—someone had.

Of course it would be Hack Orcutt. From the very first, instinct had warned Partridge that Orcutt would be a dangerous link in his plans, dangerous because of his overweening greed and a certain gross stupidity where trickery and finesse were concerned.

Yet, he had been forced to use Orcutt. Years over the gambling table had made Partridge a pretty shrewd judge of men. One by one he had measured the cattle barons of the surrounding range. And in the end he knew that Hack Orcutt was the only one he dared approach with his scheme of loot and rapine. All of the others would have shot him down on the spot had he put such a proposition to them. They were honest men and, while Partridge's secret opinion was that all honest men were fools, he knew better than to chance the wrath of their guns openly.

So he had gone to Orcutt with his proposition and Orcutt had listened, bargained—and finally agreed. Partridge had known how to handle Hack Orcutt. The promise of loot—that was it; loot in the way of cattle and range. And Orcutt had fallen victim to his greed. But Orcutt was a blunderer.

He had not been content to wait until the set-up was

ripe. He had already reached out and laid his greedy rope on Fishhook stock. And he had done it clumsily, leaving the evidence so much in the open that Cole Bridger and Red Kester had little trouble in locating the damning evidence.

Partridge realized only too well that this one little thing might bring the entire plan toppling about his ears. He had thought that plan out so carefully, step by step. First of course had been the ousting of Bill Raine as sheriff. After that a carefully maneuvered splitting up of the cattlemen. One by one they were to be removed, by fair means or foul. Those whom Partridge might bluff, he would bluff. If they proved too stubborn for this, well—there were the guns of such as Mogy Evans, and others. And as the balance of power came his way he would grow bolder, strike harder and more defiantly. It had seemed a good scheme—it was still a good scheme.

True, that move of Raine's in forming an association among the cattlemen had been unlooked for and represented a tough obstacle to overcome. But it could be done, if damn fools like Orcutt did not go on blundering. Obviously, it was high time that Orcutt was told a few things.

His mind made up on this score, Partridge headed for the Algerine. He saw the two Texans, Lon Sheer and Jim Early, standing in the shade of the false front of the saloon, watching his approach. Partridge's eyes flickered, then grew blank and opaque.

Funny the chill those two tall, still-faced fellows

gave him. In a way, unknown quantities, those two. But Partridge, who could read men, could not ignore that chill. He wished he had a score just like them on his side. Of course, he had men coming in—one group which should arrive at any time. But there was something about Sheer and Early—something about them—

As Partridge reached the shadow of the false front, Early turned to his companion. "Yuh know, Lon," he drawled—"I never thought I'd live to see the day when a human coyote would be paradin' around behind a honest sheriff's star. No sir, I never did."

Lon Sheer nodded, his glance glued on Partridge. "Nor me, Jim. Even so, that don't change the fact that the coyote is still a coyote."

It took all of Partridge's self-control to mask his feelings. But he made a job of it. He went on into the Algerine as though he had never heard. Behind him he could hear the slow, measured stride of the two Texans as they followed.

Partridge went straight to the back room. He paused a moment in the door of the room, and spoke to the bartender. "I've got to get some sleep, Joe. Send me in a drink and then see that I'm not disturbed for a few hours."

The bartender nodded and Partridge closed the door of the room behind him. A few moments later a Mexican hanger-on of the saloon came in with the desired whiskey. At Partridge's quick nod he closed the door.

"Listen, Pancho," snapped Partridge. "I've got to get out of town for a couple of hours and I don't want anyone to know I'm gone. When you go back in the barroom, stick around for a little while. Then slide out and get me a horse. You can start out of town on it, but when you get out of sight, cut around over east into that patch of brush country by Chimney Rock. I'll meet you there. That's all."

The Mexican nodded and went out. Partridge downed the drink, then went to the single window of the room and looked out. Here was the no-man's land of a cow-country town. Here a litter of rubbish—empty bottles, tin cans—the usual conglomeration of refuse which gathered at the rear of a saloon. Some twenty yards away the brush began, chemisal and greasewood, in scanty patches at first, but thickening with the distance.

Partridge slid the window open, took another look, then climbed through. A moment later he had disappeared in the brush. Half an hour later he was taking over the reins of the horse he had ordered.

"You stay right here," he told the Mexican. "I'll be back later and I'll want you to take the horse back the way you brought it."

The Mexican found a patch of shade and settled down stoically. Partridge spurred away at an angle which brought him eventually to Cottonwood Creek, where he paused a moment while his mount drank, then spurred on to the H Bar O Connected ranchhouse, reaching it just at midday.

He found Hack Orcutt at dinner with his men. At sight of Partridge, Orcutt's beefy face took on a nervous, sweaty look. He got to his feet clumsily. "Better sit up an' eat, sheriff," he mumbled.

Partridge shook his head. "Haven't time. Want to talk to you, Orcutt—alone."

Orcutt nodded, blinked and led the way into another room. Then he faced Partridge angrily. "Why in hell d'yuh have to do this?" he blurted. "If some of the other crowd see you ridin' in here to visit me they'll start puttin' two an' two together an' makin' four of it, shore as hell. If yuh had to come out, why didn't yuh wait until dark?"

Partridge's lip curled. "If I waited any longer you'd probably have the whole scheme down around my ears by that time, you greedy, stupid lunk-head. I came out here to lay the law down to you, Orcutt. I came out here to tell you not to make a single damn move until I give you the orders to. You couldn't wait, could you? You had to start tampering with Fishhook cattle. And the time wasn't nowhere near ripe. But you had to get your greedy paws on some loot. Well, here's something to chew on. Bridger and Kester are wise. That's where they were last night. They were on your Cottonwood Creek range, looking for evidence. They found it. That Raine girl visited them in jail this morning and I happen to know that they told her what they found. Also, they gave her instructions to tell her father about it."

Orcutt's pouchy, red face had gone slowly white as he listened. "Yuh're—yuh're shore of that?" he gulped.

"Too damn sure. And I had to make a move that is going to start a showdown long before I was ready for it. I knew I couldn't let that girl spread the news to her father. Not that I give a tinker's damn what would happen to you because of it. But it would jumble our plans and bring every cattle outfit around here hammering at our ears. You knew damn well what the original line of action was. It was to move carefully, smartly. It was to break up the cattlemen—pull them apart, disorganize them. Once that was done we had everything our own way. As it is—well, you've blundered into something that may be mighty hard to stop."

Orcutt was licking his lips. "But that girl—how did yuh—?"

"I've taken care of her," cut in Partridge curtly. "But having to do that will no doubt start almost as much trouble for us as letting her carry the news would. And all this because you couldn't go slow and wait."

Orcutt got some of his aplomb back. "I'm beginnin' to wish I'd never tied up in yore damn schemin', Partridge. For a cent I'd—"

"No you wouldn't," purred Partridge. "Not for a cent nor for a million dollars. For, as much as you love money, Hack Orcutt, you value your worthless life more. And if you think I'm going to run the chance of failure in this, just because of a yellow, thick-headed fool like you, you're wrong. You'll play right along with us, just as the original plans called for. You're in this up to your neck, the same as the rest of us. You'll take your chances with us—you'll win or lose with us.

And if you make one more blundering move—if you do a single thing without orders from me, or if you try and double-cross me and get out from under, your life won't be worth a plugged nickel. That's gospel—all the way. I'm playing this game to win—and I intend to do it—no matter what the cost. Understand?"

For a long moment Hack Orcutt stared at Partridge, and what he saw in the black, hard eyes of the man turned his knees to water and drenched him in the clammy sweat of fear. Orcutt swallowed and nodded.

"All right, Jay," he stammered. "I—I'm with yuh, all the way. An' I'll wait orders."

"Good enough," crisped Partridge. "I've got to be riding."

Partridge did not spare his mount on the way back to town. As he rode he cursed the necessity of having to make this ride in the first place. But Orcutt had to be ironed down and Partridge was wise enough to know that only he himself could have made the desired impression on the sulky, thick-headed cattleman. Mogy Evans might have done it, but Mogy was off on other business, business even more important.

So far, Partridge had been in luck. He was fairly sure that no one had seen him leave town. He had passed no one along the trail, going or coming. There would be no one to wonder at his errand, to start gossip which might prove embarrassing.

And then, just as he was about to swing clear of the last out-thrust shoulder of the Punch Bowl Hills, he hauled his mount to a rearing stop and cursed sound-lessly. Just in time he had glimpsed the peak of a som-brero, rising and falling to the gait of a jogging pony. The slope of the land and the skirting of brush had momentarily saved Partridge from being seen by that approaching rider, but in another fifty yards the rider would round into the clear, when discovery would be inevitable.

Momentarily Partridge hesitated. He might be able to bluff this out. But he remembered that he had given out word in the Algerine that he would be in the back room of the saloon, resting. To be met and recognized out here after that bit of strategy, might mean nothing. Again, it might arouse the very suspicion and conjec-ture that he desired, for the time at least, to allay.

His narrowed eyes stabbed from side to side. On the left there was nothing but open country. But on the right, there in the shoulder of the hills, was a narrow wash, slanting upward toward the top of the ridge, brush choked and crooked. Partridge whirled his mount and dug in the spurs.

The animal lunged up the dry-wash, splitting the brush before it. A short, scrambling effort and a turn of the wash hid both horse and rider from the trail. Par-tridge reined in, slipped to the ground and stole back until he was in position to watch. He was not entirely sure but that the sound of that quick dash into the brush had carried too far for safety. He drew a gun and waited.

The other rider jogged into view. Partridge caught his

breath in recognition. It was Jack Batten, member of the Rhyolite County Cattlemen's Association, owner of the Long Circle outfit and good friend of Bill Raine. Jack Batten, one of the very men Partridge was scheming to break and ruin.

Apparently Batten had not heard the sound of Partridge's swift scramble up the dry-wash. He rode at an easy slouch, hat pulled low against the glare of the sun, half-smoked cigarette drooping from one corner of his mouth.

But abruptly Batten reined in, staring at the trail before him. And Partridge instantly knew why. The overturned dust from his bronco's hoofs had not had time to bleach in the sun. There it was, dark evidence of a rider having passed but a minute before.

Jack Batten's head jerked up, his right hand slipping swiftly toward the holstered gun flaring at his bechapped thigh. Evil intuition whispered in Partridge's ear. There was a man whom his plans called to be broken, perhaps killed, some time. Why not now?

The gun in Partridge's hand seemed to swing level and poise of its own volition. It spat a thin, bright pencil of flame and flat, thudding report. A tiny gout of dust leaped from the back of Jack Batten's shirt. The blow knocked him forward against the horn of his saddle where he lay, twisting and writhing. Then, horribly limp, he slid loosely to the ground, while his startled horse leaped aside and swung around, snorting and stamping, its eyes fixed on the dead man in the trail.

For a moment Partridge stared down at the dread evi-

66

dence of his handiwork. At this moment he was all evil, all killer. His black eyes moiled and fumed with red flames. Then he turned back to his own horse and led it to the top of the wash and thence to the crest of the ridge. Still on foot he took a long look in every direction.

Nowhere did any movement show, except down in the trail, where Jack Batten's horse was still milling to and fro. Partridge went into the saddle and dug in the spurs. Twenty minutes later he was at the rendezvous by Chimney Rock, where the Mexican still waited.

"Give me fifteen minutes before you start back for town," he panted. "Put the horse away and rub him down, so he won't appear to have been ridden far or fast. Then come over to the Algerine and report. I've got another job for you, Pancho."

Being a methodical soul, Pancho did exactly as he was told. And he was considerably surprised, when he presented himself at the Algerine some time later, to see Partridge standing in the open door of the back room, yawning and stretching like a man who had just awakened from a deep sleep. Pancho had to pinch himself to make sure he wasn't seeing things, so perfectly did Partridge play the part, with his black hair tousled, his eyes squinty and sleepy looking.

But this appearance speedily disappeared as Partridge called for another drink and then shut the door behind Pancho as he delivered it.

"Listen close," rasped Partridge. "You know that old sheep-herder shanty on Table Mountain—the one back in the roughs? Good. Evans—Mogy Evans is out there with that Raine girl. I want you to get together a pack of grub and blankets and slide out there. Mogy will turn the girl over to you. Keep her there until you hear from me again. Understand—no rough stuff. Make damn sure she doesn't get away from you and scare the devil out of her if she gets flighty. But—no—rough stuff. Savvy?"

Pancho nodded, hiding a subdued glitter in his beady eyes. "*Sí*—señor, Pancho unnerstands. W'en you want me to leave?"

"Soon as you can get away without attracting any attention. Mogy wants to be on hand for the business tonight. That's all."

Pancho started to leave the room but, as he did so, there was a burst of movement at the front door of the saloon and a squat, bow-legged, yellow haired cowpuncher came rushing in.

"Where's that wise new sheriff of ours?" he bawled. "There's work for him out along the trail. Where is he?"

Partridge drew a hissing breath as he pushed past the Mexican and strode into the barroom. "Somebody looking for me?" he demanded curtly. "Oh—it's you, Merrick. What's on your mind?"

"Plenty, by Gawd!" panted Merrick. "There's a daid man in the trail out about three miles from town. It's Jack Batten. He's been dry-gulched, looked like to me."

An immediate hubbub followed this announcement.

Men crowded in from all sides, asking questions, arguing—morbidly curious for more details.

Pancho slid away and left the place. He had no particular interest in dead men. From all he had seen and heard in the past few weeks there would be more of them. He was thinking of that blue-eyed gringo señorita out at the sheep-herder shack on Table Mountain.

V

NORMA RAINE PARTED WITH LON SHEER AND JIM Early just outside the sheriff's office. "Yore daddy told us to stick around, Miss Norma," said Lon. "He ain't exactly trustful of that jasper, Partridge.

"There's been such things as jail deliveries an' lynchin's in this neck of the woods before this. One of them things ain't in order just now, seein' as two innocent men would be the victims. So me an' Jim are sorta keepin' a lookout in case we might be needed."

Norma nodded. "I'm awfully glad to hear you say that—about Mr. Bridger and Red Kester being innocent, I mean." She colored slightly. "I'll go and order their food and then I think I'll go on home. Dad won't be in town until late this afternoon and there is no sense in my hanging around. See you later, boys."

The two Texans watched her swing lithely along and enter the door of the little eating house. Their eyes were twinkling. "It ain't a bit hard to tell when a young lady is in love, eh, Jim?" chuckled Lon.

"Not a bit," agreed Early. "Which is plumb natural an' good, seein' that she picks a clean, square-shootin' young feller like Bridger to fall in love with. An' the funny part of it—she thinks nobody knows it but herself. But she's too plumb honest to be able to hide a secret like that. It looms up in every word she says."

When Norma had communicated her orders to the little, wrinkled-up Chinaman who ran the eating house, she went to her horse, mounted and jogged out of town. As she rode she hummed softly to herself.

Lon and Jim were right. Norma was in love and had just begun to realize it. It was the most delicious, thrilling thought she had ever known. She had actually been acquainted with Cole Bridger but a few short hours; that is, to speak to. But she had seen him at previous times and heard a lot of talk about him.

Before he had been on the Fishhook Ranch two weeks she had heard old-timers uttering gruff words of approval among themselves about Cole. A live wire, a go-getter, they called him—a young fellow who knew where he was going and how to get there.

Even then Norma had been more than ordinarily interested in him. For some reason his industry, his intelligence, his reputation of manliness attracted her. He began to take on legendary attributes, even before she had ever laid eyes upon his face.

When she finally had met him and seen the dynamic manner in which he had protected her father and herself, the deadly ferocity with which he had cut down the would-be assassin, and the magnificent noncha-lance he had displayed in scorning Jay Partridge and knocking him cold with a single punch, from that moment her heart was gone.

In the jail he really had seemed overjoyed to see her. Norma thrilled all over again at the memory of the warm pressure of his hands, the glad light in his eyes and the gentle drawl of his voice. It seemed as if—as if . . .

Norma did not go on with the thought. A movement by her bronco, a change in the regular shuffling beat of its hoofs, jerked her from her roseate reverie. She looked up and saw a rider jogging toward her down the trail. For some reason a hint of disaster came to Norma. She could not explain it, but it was there just the same. She did not recognize the approaching rider. He had his hat pulled low and his head slightly bent.

Looking around her, Norma was surprised that she had come as far from town as she had. Time and space had both flown during the concentration of her thoughts. She looked at the rider again. Apparently he had noted her presence and had reined off the trail, though not changing his pace in the slightest. Again that trickle of trepidation went up her spine.

Hiding the movement, she swiftly unbuckled the flap of the saddle bag slung across the cantle behind her. In the bag her hand settled upon the butt of a slim-bar-reled .38 Colt gun that her father had early insisted she never be without while riding alone.

The feel of the weapon reassured her. As the fellow

came opposite she looked directly at him and felt a little start of repulsion and terror. Norma recognized him as Mogy Evans, brother of the man who had tried to shoot her father in the back—and whom Cole Bridger had killed.

If Evans marked the start of fear that crossed her face, he did not show it. He looked straight at her and past her, giving no sign of recognition.

Norma heaved a sigh of relief, starting to upbraid herself as being foolish to feel such unwarranted fear. She let go of the gun and began fumbling at the buckle of the saddle bag. And then something hissed sibilantly in the air. Norma recognized it instantly and tried to flatten herself low over the saddle horn, at the same time digging in both spurs.

Too late! Even as she bent forward the accurately tossed riata settled about her shoulders and was jerked tight. The spurred bronco leaped forward and for a moment Norma thought the pull of the rope was going to drag her from the saddle.

But the man who had thrown the rope knew his business. He spurred after her, judging his pace so he could keep the rope not tight enough to drag her to the ground, but tight enough so she could not throw it off.

Recovering from the first feeling of helpless terror as the rope settled about her, Norma began struggling, trying to slip the noose and free herself. She twisted in the saddle, gaining a fraction of slack; then she spread her elbows and slipped the noose upwards. For a moment she thought she was going to make it.

Then the rope, sliding upward off her hunched shoulders, whipped tight about her throat with a terrifying stricture. The roughness of it bruised her tender flesh, and the tightness of it cut off her breath. She opened her mouth to scream, but could accomplish nothing more than a strangled gurgle.

She wavered, feeling as though she was about to reel headlong. Then a horse plunged up beside her; there was a gruff word of command, and her own mount came to a stop. The rope about Norma's neck slackened and was lifted away. A hand reached out and twitched the saddle bags free.

"Now," came a voice, flat and cold and deadly, "if yuh're willin' to listen to reason, mebbe we'll get along."

Norma, both hands massaging her bruised throat, stared at the fellow, wide of eye and accusing. "I hope," she stormed angrily, "you realize what you are doing. I hope you understand what the penalty will be for this. My father—"

"Ain't got a thing to say about it," broke in Mogy Evans roughly. "I'm runnin' this. Now then, do I have to tie yuh in yore saddle, or will yuh come along quiet and peaceable?"

Norma shivered. This fellow seemed as hard and as implacable as a prowling wolf. Frantically, her eyes searched the sunlit, smiling world about her. Nowhere was there a sign of help, of human occupancy.

"Where are you taking me?"

"Yuh'll find out when yuh arrive. Come along peaceable an' sensible, an' yuh'll be quite all right. Try raisin' a rumpus an' it'll be the worse for yuh. I'm still askin' yuh—do I have to tie yuh to yore saddle, or are yuh gonna use yore haid?"

"I'll come quietly," Norma murmured.

Now that the first shock of the encounter had passed, Norma's natural good sense and judgment were steadying her. There was nothing to be gained by further struggle and talk. Later—well, it would depend on how the chances fell.

Though she knew her captor to be a gunman and a killer, she felt that he had told her the truth when he said that she would be decently treated as long as she obeyed his orders. Besides, she knew that when her disappearance was discovered, the hunt that would follow would be relentless and dogged.

Evans took the lariat he had used to catch her with and knotted one end of it about her bronco's neck. He coiled the balance of it in his hand, then nodded towards the east, where, some eight miles distant, the abrupt face of Table Mountain lifted against the horizon.

"That way," he snapped briefly. "Lead out. Take it at a jog."

Norma obeyed without any further words. As she rode she tried to figure out the purpose behind this abduction. Inasmuch as Mogy Evans and his dead brother, Claude, had been more or less associated with Jay Partridge, she sensed the hand of the latter behind her capture. Just what he should hope to gain by such a maneuver was problematical. It would raise a storm of anger and fuming vengeance throughout the range as nothing else could.

Of course, this might be merely a stroke of vengeance against her father. Norma knew that Partridge hated her father and would glory in anything which might embarrass him or cause him loss and sorrow. As she reasoned thus, fear began trickling through her again. Assuredly some curse had fallen over the Punchbowl Hills range. The shadows were gathering.

Norma stiffened her spine and her spirit. Her head came up proudly. Whatever her fate she determined that she would not quail. She would show she was a true daughter of the West.

By this time she and this silent, slit-eyed puncher riding to one side and somewhat behind her, had entered into the apron of tangled brush country which matted the low slope in front of the gaunt, bleak palisades of weather-scarified sandstone which formed the face of Table Mountain. Norma knew that she was strictly on her own now.

There wasn't one chance in a thousand of their meeting anyone in this part of the country. This knowledge steeled her spirit, buoyed up her natural courage and set her mind to scheming. For the more she thought over the matter the more she realized that some stern purpose lay behind her capture.

This was all part of a deep-laid, nefarious scheme. To do her part to foil this scheme it would be necessary to escape. Therefore she determined to overlook no chance, however slight, to make a break for freedom.

"Turn right," came the harsh command from Mogy Evans. It was the first time he had spoken since they left the trail.

Norma did as she was bidden, her horse threading its way through the brush, traveling parallel to the face of the plateau. Presently they came to the steep sides of a ravine which emerged from a broken, narrow gorge that knifed back into the cliffs.

"Up the ravine," ordered Evans.

The way grew narrow and tortuous, but Norma saw that they were now following a faint, little used trail that wound and twisted crazily, but which had begun to climb the precipitous sides of the gorge.

The trail steepened until the horses were laboring. In places it was broad and secure. In others it became heart-shakingly narrow, crawling across the face of cliffs and around sharp angles where a misstep would have meant certain death on the rocks far below.

At length they reached the flat, plateau-like summit of Table Mountain, a wilderness of fairly level sandstone, scantily garbed with stunted brush. Norma looked around her carefully. She was searching for some kind of landmark that would aid as a guide in finding the trail down again, in case she was able to make a successful attempt at escape. She located one finally, a pile of broken-up rock to her left, with a pointed, spire-like effect at its top.

Evans now took the lead, heading slightly northeast,

apparently quite sure of his direction. For a mile he led the way across what was apparently a perfectly flat piece of plateau country. Abruptly he reined in, and as Norma's bronco came to a halt beside him, she saw that just below them was a small, cup-like hollow, about two hundred yards across.

In the center of it was a group of stunted junipers and piñons, a hint of greenery showing on the ground below. Huddled at the edge of the thicket was a cabin, incredibly warped and battered and ramshackle. Immediately Norma knew that this was to be her prison.

Evans led the way downward and across the hollow. Before the sagging door of the hut he reined in and dismounted. "Get down," he said curtly. "Here's where yuh stay."

Norma obeyed wordlessly, a feeling of desolation and loneliness coming over her. She felt terribly alone and helpless. Evans paused at the door. "Not exactly a hotel," he rasped with a tight smile. "It'll have to do, though. There'll be some food and beddin' brought in for yuh later on today."

Norma looked at the bare, ugly, rubbish-littered interior and turned away. "I prefer the open," she said quietly. Then, without another word she found a shady spot beneath the trees and sat down, making a distinct effort to preserve her attitude of calm and unconcern.

Evans busied himself unsaddling and picketing out the horses in the scanty grass that grew about the overflow of the little spring, from back in the trees. This done, he also found a seat in the shade, where he rolled himself a smoke and then began pawing over the contents of Norma's saddle bags.

Most of the various odds and ends he soon lost interest in, but that sleek little .38 Colt gun held his attention for some time. He punched out the cartridges, tested the balance of the gun, snapped it once or twice, then put it back where he had found it. But the ammunition for it he threw out into the brush.

One of the cartridges struck a limb and was deflected enough to fall near Norma's horse. Evans did not notice this, however, and Norma lowered her head to hide the quick gleam that came into her eyes. She'd remember that cartridge.

Assured that he had unloaded the gun and that no more cartridges for it remained in the saddle bags, Evans tossed the leather containers over to Norma. After that he simply sat and smoked, rolling one cigarette after another and displaying the patience of an animal.

Midday came and passed. Norma felt herself drowsing and once she did sleep for a short time. When she awoke with a start she looked quickly at Evans. He sat as before, a cigarette between his fingers, alert and watchful.

The long, hot, still hours dragged away. The sun was beginning to slant down into the west before Norma's bronco lifted its head, its ears pricked forward. Abruptly it whistled loudly, and a reply came from just beyond the rim of the hollow. Evans was on his feet in a second, his hands dropping to the butts of the two guns he carried.

A mounted man appeared on the rim, leading a well laden pack animal behind him. He halted a moment until he caught sight of them, then he waved and came on down.

Evans, apparently recognizing a friend, relaxed and went across to meet the newcomer. As the latter came toward her, Norma saw that he was a Mexican, a gross, swarthy, brutal-featured individual. Again she knew the swift flicker of fear. Was she to be left alone with such a brute? The thought frightened her.

Evans, Norma knew, was a killer and a renegade, yet she did not fear him now. He had shown no more interest in her than if she had been a stray sheep. But the moment the black, slightly bulging eyes of the Mexican rested upon her, she knew that there was a different type of renegade. She shuddered in spite of herself.

To hide her agitation she got to her feet and crossed with apparent carelessness to her bronco. With a handful of dried grass and leaves she began currying the sweat-stained animal, forcing every movement to be natural. But while she worked her eyes were swiftly searching the ground around.

Then she saw it, a single yellow cartridge, just an inert article of brass and lead and powder. But something told her that lone cartridge might mean more than life to her. She worked up about the bronco's head and neck, cleverly maneuvering the beast until it had moved so that its hind feet were less than a foot from the cartridge.

Now she worked back along the broncho's barrel and down the hind legs. A cautious glance showed her that Evans and the Mexican were busy unpacking the animal the Mexican had been leading.

A swift dart of her hand and the cartridge was safely in her palm. A thrill coursed through her. She was not whipped yet. Then Evans called her peremptorily. "Come over here."

With a final pat for her horse, Norma crossed to the two men, fighting to keep her face impassive and calm. "This is Pancho," said Evans. "He's yore jailer until further notice. As long as yuh do as yuh're told an' make no breaks at gettin' away, yuh'll be safe enough. But if yuh try a getaway yuh'll have to take the consequences. Understand?"

"I'm not deaf," replied Norma steadily. "Yes, I understand."

She met the Mexican's eyes, then looked quickly away. What a repulsive animal the fellow was! She clenched her hand so tightly about the cartridge the rim of it cut in and caused a dart of pain.

The two men busied themselves getting together a meal and, when it was cooked, Evans brought Norma a generous share. Then he returned to the fire.

Norma ate, not because she wanted to, but because she knew the wisdom of keeping up her strength for an emergency. And that such an emergency would come, she was confident. For she was determined that, before the night was over, she would have made some kind of an attempt at escape.

The guttural tones of the Mexican came to her. "Tonight you get even for your brother, eh, Mogee?"

"Plenty," grunted Evans.

"The boss says about midnight eet happen. Condon an' hees men weel be in town by then. The boss, he's show me the ropes, weeth the nooses already tied. He's wise, that hombre. He forgets nothing."

"He forgot Orcutt," snapped Evans. "Orcutt's a fool an' the boss should have known it. Orcutt grabs off some stock from the Fishhook an' blots the brands. Then what does he do but let one of the critters hang around where Bridger and Red Kester run across it an' spot that blotted brand.

"Bridger told the girl about it while she was visitin' him in jail an' she was ridin' for home to tell her father. That's why Partridge sent me out to haid her off. It's unforeseen things like that which crop up to spoil the best laid plans. From now on we'll have to move fast all around before the ranchers get organized."

"Theengs are moving fast," grunted the Mexican complacently. "First eet was Harding removed. Just before I left town the word was out that Jack Batten had got hees. Next eet weel be Ryan an' Raine. An' through the night Bridger an' Kester weel be strung up. Yes, things are moving fast."

Evans darted a quick look at Norma. Her head was bent over her plate, as though busy with her food. But the pose was to shield her eyes which were staring and horrorstruck. Had her ears tricked her?

She had known of Harding's death. Now Batten was dead. Pat Ryan and her father were next and the talk was of Cole—Cole Bridger and Red Kester being lynched before morning! It was nightmarish, almost unbelievable! But the Mexican had spoken with the ring of animal satisfaction and truth in his voice.

Evans cautioned the Mexican to lower his voice and the rest of their conversation was in unintelligible mutters. It did not matter. Norma had heard enough to turn her blood to ice and set her heart to choking her. So this was what her father had envisioned when Partridge had been elected sheriff—this wave of red ruin and death, which was to sweep the Punchbowl Hills range.

Norma saw through the whole plan now. With Partridge as sheriff the killings could be pulled off and the blame laid on innocent men. These innocent men were to be lynched before a fair trial could bring out the truth. And after the murder, there would be the sweep of rustlers and thieves. The country would be stripped bare, with crime running loose and rampant. Truly a nightmare—a terrible one!

Norma fought her feelings grimly. She still had that single cartridge. A break might come; it must come! But she had some acting to do—she had to show a measure of self-control and coolness. If she could, by some desperate ruse, make a getaway, she could ride to Baird in time to forestall this calamity. The thought thrilled her, brought back her courage, made her cool with the calmness of desperation.

As soon as the meal was finished, Evans saddled up his horse, mounted and rode off without another word or look for Norma. As she watched him go, she could sense the grim, tenacious hate which was guiding him. The fellow cared for nothing but the sating of his vengeance against Cole Bridger. Mogy Evans was riding to help with the lynching of Jay Partridge's two prisoners.

As soon as Evans had disappeared, the Mexican walked over and stood before Norma, his feet outspread, a mocking, leering grin on his repulsive face.

"So," he smirked, "the gringo señorita is alone with Pancho, eh? That ees good. She weel come to like Pancho, perhaps. It would be well eef we were friends. But I must see those saddle bags. Mogee, he told me that een them you have a gun—a gun without cartridges. I must see for myself. Perhaps eet would not be wise to trust the señorita weeth a loaded gun. She might shoot poor Pancho then." And he roared with oafish laughter.

Norma, hiding her true feelings under a mask of imperturbability, handed over the saddle bags. With eager greed the Mexican went through them. He examined the gun and made sure there were no cartridges in either it or the saddle bags. He tossed both back at her feet.

He bowed with clumsy mockery. "You see, señorita, Pancho ees not a thief. He takes nothing. He onlee makes sure." He laughed again. "And now I go to make ready for my guest," he went on. "Weel the lady sleep beneath the stars or in the cabin?"

"Bring me blankets and I will make my own bed," said Norma tersely.

The Mexican shrugged and his bulging eyes glinted at her bruskness. "So, the señorita ees unfriendly, eh? Ah, well, perhaps as the days go by she weel not be so unfriendly."

In these last words Norma sensed a meaning that again brought that chill of repulsion.

The Mexican moved away toward the pile of equipment he had brought in on his pack horse. Norma, through shaded lashes, watched him closely. Her hand went out carefully, pulling the saddle bags to her. She caught up the gun and flipped open the cylinder.

Swiftly she thrust into the chamber the lone cartridge, closed the cylinder and spun it until the cartridge would be under the hammer the next time the gun was cocked. A strange, combative urge came over her, a feeling that fairly startled her with its intensity and cold purpose.

She rose slowly to her feet and advanced toward the Mexican. He was bent over the luggage and was not aware of her proximity until she was less than ten feet from him. Then he straightened and whirled with a startled curse. He found himself looking squarely into the round, blue eye of Norma's gun!

"Put up your hands!" she said steadily. "Put them up, quick! Then turn around. If you don't do as I say I'll shoot you like I would a rattlesnake."

For a moment the Mexican half started to obey. Then

he grinned maliciously. "The señorita would joke weeth Pancho—no?" he leered. "She would shout 'boo' at heem like she would frighten a rabbit. She plays a game weeth an empty gun. Eet ees very pretty, but eet annoys me. Put the gun down. Eet ees not wise to annoy Pancho."

"You've got but a few seconds to obey," stated Norma. "The gun is not unloaded. It is ready to kill and it will kill unless you obey instantly."

The Mexican's eyes narrowed. He centered his glance on the cylinder of the threatening gun. As he did so Norma cocked the weapon, spinning the cylinder and putting that lone bullet behind the barrel and out of the Mexican's view. She saw his heavy brain and thick lips counting the empty cylinder. As far as he could see there were no cartridges in the gun.

The leering smile spread again over his face. He took a step forward. "You do not obey Pancho. For that I punish you. I shall cut a switch and whip you like I would a foolish child."

He made a sudden grab for the gun, missed it, and thrust out his hand to grab a second time. As he did so a thin, red pencil of flame licked out from the weapon. It leaped in recoil and the keen crack of it echoed hollowly over the little basin.

Paralysis gripped the Mexican. He stood like some awkward statue, his talon paw still outstretched, the leering grin still on his face. Only the expression of his eyes had changed and into them came a vast and ludicrous look of surprise.

For a moment the expression held. Then his eyelids fluttered, he gaped a meaningless word, his knees buckled and he pitched forward on his face. That lone cartridge had done its work. It had hurled its leaden missile straight to the Mexican's heart.

Five minutes later, Norma Raine spurred up out of the basin, riding low and hard—a fleeting shadow through the rapidly thickening dusk.

VI

Bill Raine was on his way to town to meet the afternoon stage, when he heard the news of Jack Batten's killing. It came from the lips of Lon Sheer, whom Raine had met heading for the home ranch at a furious gallop.

At sight of his square-jawed, grizzle-haired boss, Lon reined in with what sounded strangely like an exclamation of huge relief. Raine looked at the tall, grave-faced Texan in some surprise.

"What's the rush, Lon," he asked, as Lon brought his bronco to a rearing halt beside him. "Trouble in town?"

"Not in town—outside of it," said Lon tersely. "They just found Jack Batten, shot in the back. Dry-gulched. Never had a chance for his alley."

Raine stiffened in astonishment and swiftly growing rage. "Jack Batten? Daid? Lon, yuh ain't jokin'?"

"Nary a joke, Bill. Spud Merrick of Pat Ryan's Cross-in-a-Box outfit was haidin' for town just after

86

dinner. About three miles out he ran across a riderless hoss, amblin' along the trail. Spud recognized the critter as that mouse roan geldin' that Batten rides most of the time.

"Spud roped the bronc an' looked things over. He found bloodstains on the saddle so he started back-trackin' the sign left by the roan. It took him straight to Batten's body. Pore ole Jack had been shot in the back an' was piled up under a mesquite bush, daid as a mackerel. Both Jack's guns were still in the leather an' neither of 'em had been fired.

"It was murder, Bill, cold-blooded and pre-medi-tated. Knowin' yuh was ridin' in to town this after-noon, Jim an' me talked things over an' decided I better come along an' see that yuh were all right. Jim's stickin' in town to watch things like yuh ordered."

For a time Raine was speechless. His face turned cold and grim and terrible. "Thanks, Lon," he said harshly. "I appreciate the thought an' action. I believe yuh're right at that. Harding first, now Batten. It looks like a hell-born scheme to clean all us ole-timers out. It'll pay me to ride slow an' watch my step. What did Partridge have to say about Batten's killin'?"

Lon laughed mirthlessly. "He arrested Spud an' chucked him in jail. Then he went out with a spring wagon to bring in Batten's body."

"But why in the name of all things holy should he arrest Spud?" exploded Raine.

"You tell me an' I'll tell you," answered Lon. "At that it looks to me like he's makin' a daid give-away of

87

his hand. Anybody with a lick of sense would know that Spud didn't kill Batten. Why should he? An' if he did, why would he come in town an' report it?

"Looks to me like Partridge is tryin' to swing suspicion onto innocent men for these killin's. Which means, to my way of reasonin', that he's the man that's orderin' 'em. Me, I'm goin' to run that hunch into a hole. The very next chance I get I'm callin' Partridge, forcin' his hand an' then rockin' him off on a lead lullaby. Nobody is safe as long as he's alive."

"I'm gonna have a showdown talk with that jasper as soon as I get to town," declared Raine. "C'mon, let's ride."

The town of Baird was seething with excitement and conjecture when Raine and Lon Sheer reached it. Word had gotten around of Jack Batten's murder and every minute brought more punchers riding in. Both sides of the single street were lined with horses and there was a particularly large group of them in front of the Algerine Saloon.

Jim Early came stalking up to Raine and Lon Sheer as they dismounted. His grave, still face was impassive, but there was a cold, icy look in his eyes. "There'll be blood on the moon tonight, boss," he said simply. "Lon, yuh remember Flash Condon, the Flash Condon we run outa the Staked Plains country back in the old days?"

"I shore do, Jim," answered Lon quickly. "What about him?"

Jim nodded toward the crush of horses in front of the

Algerine. "He's in town, with about two dozen of the toughest, hardest-lookin' mugs yuh ever laid eyes on. They all came in together an' Partridge, who had just got back with Batten's body, seemed tickled to death to see 'em. Him an' Flash Condon shook hands like old friends. They're all in the Algerine now, liquorin' up."

Lon Sheer's hands dropped to the butts of his guns, half drew the weapons, then choked them back into the leather. It was a swift, smooth, involuntary action. He turned to Raine.

"Bill," he drawled evenly, "I reckon it's high time that yuh got yore association members organized an' ready for war; that is, what there are left of 'em. The writin' on the wall is plain. Yore life, Pat Ryan's life an' that of Frenchy Gaston ain't worth four bits right now.

"The scheme is openin' up. They're workin' to wipe out all of yuh. They'll do it, too, unless we take the play away from 'em. There's Scotty Ladd an' Whip O'Conner of the Cross-in-a-Box. Better call 'em over an' send 'em out to spread the word. . . . Hi, Scotty and Whip—come over here, will yuh?"

Scotty Ladd and Whip O'Conner came hurrying across the street. Scotty was a little, wiry puncher with eyes the color and warmth of glacial ice. Whip O'Conner was a big, freckled, flaming-haired Irishman and the lust for combat just now lay hot in his blue eyes.

"Hell's due to roll, boys," said Raine quietly. "Will yuh do me a favor?"

"If it's somethin' to do with breakin' the back of this damned murtherin' bunch of spalpeens what's dry-gulchin' good men an' jailin' innocent ones, we're with yuh to a finish, Bill," growled Whip, a trace of his native brogue breaking into his speech, due to his wrought-up condition.

"Then hit leather an' see that Pat Ryan an' Frenchy Gaston come ridin', with all their men an' plenty of fightin' equipment. Tell Pat an' Frenchy to meet me in Hoskins' store. Will yuh do it?"

"An' how," snapped Scotty Ladd. "C'mon, Whip. We're travelin' places an' doin' things. See yuh later, Bill."

The two punchers spurred out of town. Raine turned to Lon and Jim. "Let's go up to Hoskins' place. We'll probably find Norma there. I want to get her outa town before the war starts."

Jim and Lon started. Their eyes grew bleak as death itself. "Bill," said Lon, and his voice was flat and tone-less, "didn't Miss Norma get home or pass yuh on the trail? She left town hours ago."

Bill Raine stood very still. For a long time he did not move. When he finally spoke his words were jerky and emotionless. "She never got home and she wasn't nowhere along the trail. I'm seein' Partridge—now!"

He turned and began striding swiftly for the Algerine. Lon Sheer leaped forward and caught him by the arm. "Steady, Bill. Let's think this over a little. To go in that joint now means certain death for yuh. Partridge would jump at the chance to frame yuh. They'd kill yuh without givin' yuh a ghost of a chance. Let's talk a little. Mebbe Miss Norma took a short cut or somethin'."

Bill Raine was completely past all reasoning now. He fought Lon furiously to get away. He could think of but one thing, and that was to face Jay Partridge and cut him down with hot lead. "I'll tear his heart out with my hands," he raved. "If he's harmed even one hair of my girl's haid— Lemme go, Lon—lemme go."

Lon shook his head. "Later, Bill—not now. Yuh'll spoil everythin' if yuh blow up too soon. Partridge is organized; he's got plenty of men behind him. To fight him successfully we got to do the same thing. Now I want yuh to promise me that yuh'll go to Hoskins' an' stay there until me an' Jim get back. An' while yuh're there, proposition Hoskins for the sale of every gun an' every ca'tridge in the whole place. Listen to reason, will yuh?"

Raine calmed slowly. Presently he nodded. "Okeh, Lon. Yuh're right, and I'll do as yuh say."

Lon and Jim walked with him as far as the store and saw him safely inside. Then they hurried to their mounts, leaped into the saddles and spurred away on the home trail.

They said nothing. There was no need for words. These two had worked together so long that understanding between them was complete enough without words. Each knew how the other felt.

Pacing restlessly back and forth across the narrow confines of the jail, Cole Bridger was doing a lot of concentrated thinking. He had gotten Spud Merrick's story of how he had found the dead body of Jack Batten beside the trail and the subsequent happenings that had ended by Spud being thrown into the lockup by Partridge on the charge of having murdered Batten.

Spud was fit to be tied. He had stormed and ranted and cursed until the very lack of breath had forced him to silence. Now he sat dejectedly upon a bunk, a short, stocky, bow-legged figure, with a tousled thatch of yellow hair, round, sun-reddened face and guileless blue eyes. Cole and Red Kester had commiserated with him. They knew the rankling of injustice themselves.

Cole ceased his pacing abruptly and turned to Red. "Did it ever strike yuh, Red, that the chances are long of us gettin' a trial?" he demanded.

"Plenty," growled Red. "There's somethin' in the air, Cole. I can sorta feel it. Call it a hunch or anythin' yuh want, but I'm bettin' we'll never get a chance to stand up before a jury an' tell our stories. I tell yuh I can sense a lynchin' comin' up with you an' me—an' mebbe Spud as the main characters."

"I've got the same hunch," nodded Cole. "Which means that it's high time we start doin' somethin' besides sittin' quiet here an' feelin' sorry for ourselves."

Red got to his feet from the bunk he had been lounging morosely on. His eyes were gleaming. "Yuh mean we begin figgerin' ways an' means of breakin' loose?"

"I don't say nothin' else," declared Cole. "Bill Raine means well in gettin' a lawyer for us, but I can see now that book-law is gone from these parts for a while. The law of the fang is all that's left. If Partridge shows in here again, we make a break. We'll tackle him somehow. In the meantime, I'm gonna batter somethin' loose in this joint if it's the last thing I ever do on earth. Are yuh with us, Spud?"

"All the way, Cole," grunted Spud, straightening up. "Yeah, all the way. I'd rather be plugged tryin' for a getaway any time than do a bit of rope stretchin'. Where do we start?"

"On one of these bunks. Let's see if we cain't twist a laig off one of 'em an' make a club."

A bunk was quickly opened and torn apart. Tremendous strength lay in Spud Merrick's squatty body, and he was not long in warping free several pieces of the soft steel framework.

Cole tore a blanket in pieces and wrapped a strip of cloth about one end of the longest and heaviest clubs produced by Spud's furniture smashing efforts. Gripping the cloth-covered end of the crude, but effective tool, Cole walked up to the door, squared himself and began battering away at the heavy wood around the lock.

The impact of the blows reverberated loudly, but Cole did not worry. He was convinced by this time that Partridge never had meant that he and Red should come to trial. Nor Spud Merrick either, for that matter. But if they should be spirited away and lynched during the night, many people would be convinced of their guilt and the matter let drop.

Victims would have been produced to sate the public's desire for vengeance and everybody would be happy except the victims. It was an old game and one that had been used before by unscrupulous politicians. Therefore, Cole was determined to bring matters to a head as soon as possible. Like Spud, he preferred hot lead any time to the ignominy of a noosed rope.

When Cole grew weary of his efforts, Red Kester took his place and after Red, Spud Merrick did his part. The wood of the door began to splinter and give. Cole complimented Spud enthusiastically. "We're makin' progress," he stated encouragingly. "If nobody hears this racket and we're left alone for half an hour we'll be free men."

But that muffled pounding did not pass unnoticed. During a lull in the riotous tumult in the Algerine, the sound carried to Jay Partridge's alert ears, and with Flash Condon, he ran out of the saloon and across to his office and jail.

"Those prisoners have guessed what's in store for them and are forcing the issue, Flash," snapped Partridge. "You go back to the Algerine and organize your men for the rush on the jail and the lynching. To make it look halfway right, I'll come out on the steps and make a show of talking you off.

"But I won't shoot and you have the boys appear to rush me and take my gun and keys. The rest will be simple. You'll find the ropes already cut and noosed in the cupboard in the corner of the office. Make it fast. I'll go in and try and bluff those fellows into subjection."

Flash Condon nodded and went back to the saloon. He was a sleekly built, average-sized individual, carried two guns tied down and had a pair of greenish eyes that made an observer think of a cat. His face was narrow and hard and depraved. He had gotten his nickname from his speed with a gun.

Partridge hurried into his office and, after listening at the first door, unlocked it. Even in the dim light of the narrow hall he could see that the inner door was beginning to give before the furious attack upon it. It was creaking ominously and already a ragged, splintery hole was showing just above the lock. In another minute or two it would give way completely.

Partridge drew his automatic and slipped off the safety. "Far enough in there," he yelled. "Back away from that door or I sift lead into you!"

The answer Spud Merrick gave was unprintable. Spud's efforts at the door had worked him to a state of feeling where he would have tackled a panther with his bare hands. He took a firmer grip on his battered club and began wielding it anew.

Partridge's eyes narrowed as he lifted his automatic and pumped a bullet through the door. As the report thundered, Spud Merrick gasped, staggered back, and slumped to the floor, his hands pressed against his side. Quick as a cat, Cole leaped and dragged him out of line, just in time to avoid a second slug from Partridge's gun.

"Keep back, Red," warned Cole. "Spud—Spud, ole feller, where'd that damned polecat hit yuh?"

Spud's face was white and still. He was unconscious. Cole bared the wound and saw at a glance that it was very serious, if not fatal. He went cold all over, cold with a chill, icy rage that tore at him like a living agony.

"It's bad, Red," he snapped. "Grab his feet—easy. We gotta get him on one of the bunks. Pore old Spud. I'd like a chance to get my hands on that rat of a Partridge!"

Partridge, listening by the shattered door, smiled thinly. "Maybe you jaspers will get over the idea that I'm fooling," he called. "Keep away from this door or you'll get it next. I'm telling you something."

Cole whirled and leaped close to the door, but far enough to one side that Partridge could not hit him if he tried another shot. "Yeah?" answered Cole silkily. "An' I'm tellin' you somethin', yuh yellow coyote.

"Yuh think yuh're ridin' high an' easy now, but yore game won't work. Yuh'll have to face the music, sooner or later, an' when yuh do I know yuh'll squeal like the rat yuh are. Open this door an' step in here an' I'll take yuh on, my bare hands against yore gun, yuh creepin', poisonous snake!"

There was a method in the torrent of invective Cole was pouring out. He hoped to enrage Partridge enough to cause the fellow to burst in, intent on shooting him down. The way Cole felt now he would have welcomed the chance to brave a dozen guns just to get his hands on Partridge. But his plan got little result.

Partridge laughed mockingly. "Get it off your chest, Bridger," he called. "You ain't got long. Maybe you'll talk different with a noose around your neck. You'll know the feel of a rope before very long. In the meantime, keep away from this door."

Red Kester, his eyes flaming, was ready to begin a new assault upon the weakened portal, but Cole waved him back. "No use," he shrugged. "He'd pot yuh like a rabbit, Red. They ain't got a rope around our necks yet. It'll be time to go out fightin' when they do."

As his prisoners quieted down, Partridge went back into his office and looked across at the Algerine. He found himself wishing uneasily that Condon would hurry up with the mob. Despite his pseudo-confidence and temporary position of mastery, Partridge could not get over the deadly menace that was in Cole Bridger's voice and warning.

Partridge was playing for big stakes and he realized perfectly that almost any risk was worth the gamble. But he knew that the fury of these men he had wronged would be devastating if ever allowed to get the upper hand. He snapped the end off a black perfecto, lit it, and fell to pacing back and forth across his office.

VII

DUSK THICKENED, SHROUDING IN VELVETY BLACKNESS the hate and simmering tumult of the town of Baird. Before the door of the Algerine Saloon a group of men were forming. They were shouting and cursing as they milled around, inflamed with liquor and the haranguing of Flash Condon and Mogy Evans, who had appeared shortly before.

Three hard-riding figures pounded up the street, whirled to a halt before Hoskins' store and slid to the ground. Swiftly they darted from sight into the store and a moment later Norma Raine was in her father's arms.

Old Bill's eyes were moist as he hugged her. "Honey—honey," he mumbled, "where yuh been? What happened to yuh?"

Norma struggled free. "Never mind that part now," she panted. "But listen to what I know. They're going to lynch Cole Bridger and Red Kester tonight. Hack Orcutt is in with Partridge and Partridge has some outside gang of rustlers and hard eggs who are coming in to help him clean this range right down to the bone. Partridge had Tim Harding and Jack Batten killed.

"Dad, you and Pat Ryan and Frenchy Gaston are slated to be killed also. Oh, that beast of a Partridge is mad—insane. He thinks because he is sheriff he can

98

get away with these things. Quick! We've got to get Cole and Red Kester out of jail immediately. Even now the mob is forming up by the Algerine. We saw them as we came into town."

Lon Sheer and Jim Early, who had met Norma along the trail as she came riding in from her successful escape, nodded concurrence to this. Lon stepped forward, the light of an idea in his eyes.

"Hoskins, gimme a couple of six-guns and plenty of ammunition. Mebbe Partridge is so damned confident of himself he won't be watchin' the back of that jail. If he ain't, I'm slippin' those boys some fightin' tools. Trot 'em out quick!"

Ezra Hoskins, weazened and gray, but with the fighting iron of he-man heritage in his veins, produced the guns and ammunition without a word. Lon caught them up and started for the door. Jim Early fell in behind him. "I'll be guardin' yore back, Lon," he drawled.

"Bill," ordered Jim, as he turned to Raine, "get this store ready for a fight. Build barricades—lay out guns and shells. We'll make this place the headquarters for the right crowd. Pat Ryan an' Frenchy oughta be comin' in pretty quick with their punchers. It'll be a go to the finish an' we wanta be organized right."

As the two tall, grim-faced Texans slipped outside, Hoskins and Raine exploded into activity. The two old men lugged barrels of provisions and sacks of flour and sugar to make barricades. Norma wiped grease from new Winchesters and Colt six-guns and laid them along the counter with opened boxes of ammunition, ready for action.

Lon and Jim went directly across the street, slipped down a black alley and circled to the rear of the jail. They crept up warily, but were not accosted. Evidently Partridge was too confident of his power and the malignant forces with him, to figure a rear guard of the jail as necessary.

Crouched under one of the tiny windows, Lon listened. Inside he could hear someone groaning, then the low murmur of voices. He rose to his full height. "Bridger," he called softly. "Bridger, are yuh all right? This is Sheer speakin'—Lon Sheer."

There was an exclamation of surprise and Cole came to the window. "Me an' Red are all right. Spud Merrick is wounded an' in a bad way. Partridge shot through the door at him when we was makin' a play at a getaway. Things look bad. Partridge as good as told us he was gonna see that we were lynched before mornin'."

Lon grunted non-committally. "He's due for a surprise, Bridger. Here's a couple of guns an' some ammunition for you an' Red. Make a fight of it, cowboy. Don't let anyone get into the jail. Long as yuh're in there they cain't touch yuh. Help's comin'. Pat Ryan an' Frenchy Gaston will be in with all their punchers.

"I see that Mig Almada an' Foxy an' Sad of yore outfit is in town. We're organizin'. We'll give Partridge more than he bargained for by mornin'. Keep a stiff upper lip, an' hold the fort. Get set; I can hear that mob comin'."

Lon slipped swiftly away and he and Jim circled back to the store.

Inside the jail tense, savage satisfaction gripped Cole Bridger and Red Kester. As he loaded his weapon Red began whistling softly through his teeth. His eyes rested on Spud Merrick's unconscious face, now but a pale blur through the thickening darkness.

"They'll pay, Spud, ole feller," he muttered. "A dozen for one. Yuh bet they'll pay. Partridge, yuh damned sidewinder, come an' try to get us now."

Cole said nothing, but in his heart he was echoing Red's sentiments grimly. A new confidence—a new certainty of power swayed him. He would have fought ferociously before; he would fight more so now. And he knew Red Kester would be right beside him to a bitter finish.

The voice of the mob carried to them, a heavy, ominous roar that was sinister and threatening. It was not unlike the note of an approaching storm, berserk, unreasonable, unthinking. Cole knew that once he and Red were in the hands of that faction, their finish would be sure and swift.

He rolled and lit a cigarette. "Sounds tough, eh, Red?" he drawled.

Red smiled thinly as he spun his six-gun on one brown forefinger. "They'll all be changin' their tune shortly."

The tumult outside deepened and swelled. Cole and

Red could distinguish different voices now. Like a raging sea, the mob rolled up about the front of the jail and began calling to Partridge to come out and surrender himself and his prisoners.

The howling of the mob died away somewhat. It seemed to Cole that he could make out another voice—the voice of Partridge, haranguing the crowd. But in a moment that voice was shouted down and the mob struck the place in a rush that carried them into the sheriff's office.

Cole suddenly holstered his gun, caught up the battered chunk of bar that Spud had been working with when shot down and with several lusty blows enlarged the hole in the door enough to allow the muzzle of a six-gun to cover the narrow expanse of the hall. He dropped the bar, drew his gun anew and waited.

"We'll take turns at shootin', Red," he ordered. "That way one of us will always be loaded an' ready. I'll give 'em plenty of lead soon as they come into the hall."

Cole threw away his cigarette and waited. Raucous yells of triumph echoed from the office. "Here's the ropes," howled someone. "All noosed an' ready. C'mon, let's get 'em. Open that door."

There was a moment of fumbling delay, then the first door slammed open and the narrow hall shook with the surge of trampling feet and jostling bodies. Cole pushed the muzzle of his gun through the opening and emptied it, shooting rapidly.

The roaring discharges in the small confines drowned out every other sound. There was no chance of Cole's lead going astray. If it missed one man it hit another. For one stunned, awful second the voice of the mob was stilled.

In the hall men were going down, choking and cursing, bewildered and dying. Where they had expected no further resistance than that of unarmed, helpless men, they had run up against a blast of lead that had made a shambles of the hallway. They drew back momentarily, shaken and sobered with surprise and fear.

Swiftly Cole punched the empty shells from his gun and reloaded. He motioned Red out of line with the door. "Get back," he warned softly. "There'll be lead in plenty comin' through there."

He was right. The maddened mob sent volley after volley ripping through the heavy door. Splinters whined through the air and the battered lead chugged sullenly into the back wall of the little jail. Grimly impassive of face, but keenly watchful, Cole and Red waited for the shooting to cease.

It did so presently and there came another blind rush down the hall. It was Red who now poured a furious fire along the choked passageway. Again the charge died out and the cries of stricken men rose above the sullen mutter of the mob.

Cole drew Red back into a corner. "They won't be tryin' that same rush the third time," he said softly. "From now on they'll work the windows for all they're worth. Watch 'em close. I'll go over in this opposite corner. We can take care of everythin' that way."

Momentary silence settled down, at least a comparative silence after the uproar of the past five minutes. But this diminishing of noise did not deceive Cole. He knew that now the mob was infinitely more dangerous and menacing than ever. Before it had been merely a blind, gross, unreasoning chaos of brute force, that was inflamed by profane words and liquor—a crowd drunkenly obsessed with brutality and the hunger to see helpless men die.

Now, however, it had begun to think. Those two blind charges along the hall, which had been literally blasted to a standstill by life-taking lead, had cleared the liquor fumes from the members of the mob. Now they would be slinking, vengeful, sly—maneuvering from every angle to get at the prisoners.

Proof of Cole's surmise was not long in coming. There was a sound of cautious movement outside the windows. "Get down on yore knees, Red," muttered Cole.

There were two windows on each side of the jail and one in back. From the five of them lashed pencils of flame, snarling reports and vicious lead that raked the room from all angles. Due to the height of the windows none of the attackers depressed the muzzles of their guns enough, and in consequence all of the lead flew too high to strike the prisoners.

Several times this occurred, with Cole and Red holding their fire and remaining very still. Presently the shooting stopped. In the momentary silence that fell, Spud Merrick moved slightly and groaned.

Someone outside heard it and gave a yell of exultation. "We winged 'em—we winged 'em!"

Cole's eyes were probing the window through which this yell came. Dark as it was, he caught the outline of a man's head against the subdued glow of the newly budded stars. His gun snapped up and roared. The head disappeared and there was the muffled thud of a falling body.

Immediately the full fury of the mob took voice again. Answering fire came through the windows once more and now, with the reckless fury of fighting men getting the upper hand, Cole and Red began tossing caution to the wind. They raked each window with lead, shooting carefully and effectively. The shooting from outside was stilled.

The fury of the attacking mob grew. Every attempt they had made to get at the prisoners had been abortive and costly in life to themselves. "Burn the devils out," yelled someone. "This damn jail's no good anyhow. Burn 'em out!"

The idea took immediate favor. Cole and Red could hear someone shouting for wood and coal oil. "This is gonna be tough, Red, ole-timer," drawled Cole. "I knew they'd come to that idea sooner or later. This place will burn like tinder. We're gonna have to make a break for it. I hope the folks outside who are for us will get into action pretty soon."

"Well," grunted Red stoically, "I won't care if I am toasted or leaded up now, boss. We shore evened up for pore Spud. Only thing that gets me—I'd die plumb happy if I knew Partridge had got his."

"He's probably quite safe and sound," said Cole. "He ain't the kind to take chances when he can send some ignorant, half-drunk puncher out to do it for him."

They could hear men moving and shuffling about outside. There came a swishing sound and then the raw, pungent odor of kerosene twitched at their nostrils.

"Okeh," growled a voice. "Touch it off."

A match snapped and instantly there came the rush of flame, as the kerosene ignited and took hold. Smoke began to pour into the room. Cole slid over to the bunk on which Spud Merrick lay and lifted him upon his shoulder. "Can yuh force that door, Red?" he asked quietly. "It's our only chance."

Red's answer was to hunch his shoulder and drive against the splintered door like a battering ram. It creaked and complained, but held—throwing Red back. He gathered himself and charged again, berserk fury filling him with wild, mad strength.

There came a queer, muffled snap and Red involuntarily gasped. But his effort was successful. The door smashed open, and, lurching and cursing like a madman, Red led the way over a carpet of dead men who had fallen in the two useless charges along the hall.

A lamp flickered smokily upon the sheriff's desk, but the room was empty, except for a renegade who had been fatally wounded in the hall and had crept out into the office to die. Evidently the mob had realized that the office would go up in flames with the jail, and go quickly. All of the mob had gathered outside to watch the prisoners die.

There was a queer, white set about Red Kester's lips and his left shoulder sagged loosely. At first Cole did not see it, but as he stood up after lowering the unconscious Spud upon the desk, he took note of that limply swinging arm.

"Red! Yuh're wounded. When did it happen? Lemme look at it, man."

Red shook his torchy head. "Yuh cain't do nothin' with it now, Cole. I broke my shoulder when I knocked that damn door down."

Cole's eyes flashed in admiration. "Yuh're a man, ole-timer. Sit down an' take it easy. We ain't scotched yet. They'll be watchin' the door. But if yuh remember, this office is set up from the ground quite a ways. We're goin' burrowin'.'"

Red sank into a chair, beads of cold sweat gleaming on his face. Cole went to work furiously. He darted back into the smoke-filled jail and returned with that precious bar of metal that had hammered the door to pieces. Selecting a place where a warped board had made a good-sized crack in the office floor, he jammed one end of the bar through and pried upward.

The floor board splintered and gave. Grabbing it with his hands, Cole ripped it free. He dropped it and dug after another. In a moment or two a dark hole yawned in the floor, big enough for them to get through.

"You first, Red," he ordered crisply, flicking the sweat from his eyes. "I'll bring Spud."

Grimly fighting back the sickening torture of his broken shoulder, Red Kester slid through the hole. Cole swung Spud Merrick after him and slipped downward himself. And as he did so there came the roar and rumble of hoofs down the street of Baird.

The shrill, high-pitched yells of fighting cowpunchers rose ascendant above the mutter of the mob. Pat Ryan, Frenchy Gaston and the fighting men from their ranches, together with those from Bill Raine's and Cole's, were on the job at last.

Crouching for a moment beneath the office floor, Cole heard a thunder of gunfire break out. He knew that the mob would have plenty of other things to think of now, besides roasting some defenseless men.

Hope and courage flowed through him anew. He inched along behind Red, dragging the limp bulk of Spud Merrick with him. The foundation of the building was unboarded on the sides and, in another minute, Cole and Red drew themselves erect—free men at last!

Cole got Spud on his shoulder again. "Up the street an' then 'way back of those buildin's, Red, Partridge's gang are still behind the jail, waitin' to find our charred bodies," Cole said. "Accordin' to Lon Sheer the folks will be makin' their big stand in Hoskins' place. We'll go clear around and come up to the store from in back."

They started on through the night, well away from the circle of light caused by the mounting flames that licked up the walls of the jail. The street of Baird was a battlefield now.

The mob was broken up, most of it concentrated in the Algerine Saloon. Here and there isolated members of it clung to dark pockets about the corners of buildings, swapping lead with the vengeful punchers, who were rushing to the burning jail.

Only once were Cole and Red accosted. Two men came hurrying out of the darkness towards them, men whom Red instantly identified by the question they flung at him. "Where the devil is Condon and Partridge? There's a hundred punchers seems like come into town. Things ain't healthy for us. Where is Condon?"

Red snapped up his gun as he answered. "In hell—I hope. Yuh can talk it over with him there."

And Red's two shots cut the fellows down ruthlessly. Ten minutes later Red and Cole staggered up to the rear of Hoskins' store, hammered on the door, announced their identity and were among friends.

VIII

Exultation gripped the members of the defending force who were grouped in the store. "Hell's heat!" bawled Bill Raine. "We thought you fellers would be half roasted by now. Ryan an' Gaston an' the rest of the gang shore got here just in time. How'd yuh get out?"

"Oh, one way an' another," smiled Cole grimly. "Them guns what Lon slipped us shore put a different complexion on things. But Spud here is wounded bad an' Red broke his shoulder, smashin' down a door."

Blankets were dragged from shelves and couches made for Spud and Red. Red tried to object, swearing that he could still do a lot of fighting; but Cole, cussing the iron-hearted cow-puncher affectionately, forced him to submit to rest and care.

Norma, who had been wordless since Cole's arrival, stood close beside him. "Oh, Cole," she whispered. "Cole, I've been terribly afraid."

Cole looked at her and saw that her eyes were wet. His arm went around her slim shoulders and gave them a mighty squeeze. "Yuh're all wool an' a yard wide, Norma," he told her softly. "Don't yuh weep no more. You an' me are gonna find a lot of peace an' sunshine an' happiness when this thing is over with.

"Buck up, little lady. Do the best yuh can for Spud an' Red while I get into the scrap with the other boys. Soon as I can locate him, I'll send Doc McCool over here."

Swiftly he cupped her face between his hands and, as swiftly he bent, his lips brushing hers in a magical contact which left both of them a little bewildered and breathless.

"There'll be more of that—later on," he drawled softly, and then he was gone. He went up to the front of the store, where Lon Sheer and Jim Early were crouched over two hot-barreled Winchesters.

Cole gripped Lon on one brawny shoulder. "Much obliged for those guns yuh slipped us, ole-timer," he said quietly. "They shore saved our skins. Now, what d'yuh say we get outside an' help the other boys at their job of rat exterminatin'?

"I'll locate Mig an' Foxy an' Sad an' send 'em up here to take care of any attack on the store that might come. Me, I'm huntin' Partridge an' Condon, an' I'd like you two fellers with me."

Lon and Jim exclaimed with satisfaction. *"Bueno!"* grunted Lon. "That shore listens good to me, Cole. Jim an' me don't like this kind of fightin'. We like to get out in the open where we can work right. Let's drift."

After a swift look outside, Cole left the store at a crouching run, with Lon and Jim at his heels. He saw immediately that the renegade crowd had been thoroughly dispersed and scattered. However, quite a group of them were in the Algerine, the doors and windows of which were spitting lead continually.

Cole yelled an alarm. He knew that the punchers would suffer terrible losses if they tried to rush the saloon. "Wait!" he shouted. "Hold on. This is Bridger speakin'. We got out all okeh. Come over here, all of yuh. We'll smoke the pole-cats out, but we'll take our time doin' it."

There was an answering whoop of surprise and the punchers came racing up the street. Mig Almada, Foxy and Sad were the first to reach Cole and pound him on the back in enthusiastic relief. Then came Scotty Ladd and Whip O'Conner, along with Pat Ryan and Frenchy Gaston.

Cole explained in a few brief words how he and Red Kester and Spud Merrick had escaped from the burning jail. "Foxy," he ended, "you an' Sad go to the store an' stay there. Somebody's got to guard the place an' it might as well be you two. Suppose the rest of us draw up to the other end of the street where those jaspers in the Algerine cain't snipe at us, an' hold a pow-wow."

"That's good judgment," broke in Pat Ryan. "Bridger's talkin' sense. Up the street, you fellers."

They moved away, passing out of range of the Algerine. As they went by the store, Foxy and Sad, disappointed but obedient, slipped into the doorway.

Cole turned to Mig Almada. "Mig, see if yuh can locate Doc McCool an' get him over to the store. Spud an' Red have got to have medical attention as soon as possible."

Mig nodded and went prowling off on this mission. Cole marshaled his forces in back of the livery stable. Pat Ryan and Frenchy Gaston, though much older than Cole, sensed that matters could not be left in more able hands than those of Bridger, so they tacitly turned control over to him. Cole rolled and lit a cigarette as he faced the crowd.

"I reckon this county has begun to realize that it ain't safe to neglect the duty of votin'," he drawled. "We left the gate open an' a herd of coyotes crawled in. Now it's up to us to fumigate an' set things right once more.

First of all, I might as well tell yuh that Hack Orcutt an' his gang is in this mess with Partridge, hook, line an' sinker."

A slight rumble of protest interrupted him. Cole smiled thinly and held up his hand for silence. "I know that sounds like a strong statement to a lot of you boys who've known an' drank an' rode with the H Bar O Connected gang. But it's the truth, just the same. If yuh notice, Orcutt an' his crowd ain't present tonight helpin' to clean house, are they?

"Another thing, Red Kester an' me found out for certain the night Tim Harding was killed, that Orcutt has been rustlin' my stock an' blottin' brands. One thing more, Orcutt was ridin' alone with Harding when Tim was shot down an' we can believe Orcutt's story if we want to.

"Me, I think he's lyin'. I know he is as far as connectin' Red an' me with that killin'. I'm tellin' yuh this so that yuh'll all know just who yore friends are an' where to look for enemies. We cain't use any halfway measures in this. It's whole hawg or none. Any who disagree with me might as well speak up now."

Cole paused. The crowd shifted nervously. "Yuh seem to know what yuh're talkin' about, Bridger," said someone. "I'm with yuh to a wire-edged finish."

There was a growl of concurrence with this statement. Cole went on. "Okeh, boys. Yuh'll find in the last showdown that I'm right. The killin' of Harding an' Jack Batten oughta convince any open-minded man which way the arrow is pointin'. Partridge has been schemin' this thing out for a long time.

"He figgered that by pullin' enough crooked politics to get himself elected, he could use the law to cover up his tracks an' justify every move he made. Orcutt has probably been promised his share of the loot. Flash Condon an' his crowd of thieves has been brought in to help."

"I been thinkin' things over," came Pat Ryan's voice. "Bridger has got this thing figgered correct. We'll shore ride with him."

"Thanks, Pat," nodded Cole. "Then that is settled. Now for a scheme of battle. So far, we've come off better than even. But that crowd ain't licked.

"I ain't a bloodthirsty man, but I believe in fightin' the devil with his own tools. If we surround the Algerine we oughta be able to starve that gang into submission. We got 'em where the hair's short. Their ammunition won't last forever an' they cain't live on the Algerine's supply of liquor. We got all of Ezry Hoskins' store to draw on. Now here's my idee.

"We split up into four gangs. Pat can take one, Frenchy another, Lon an' Jim another an' I'll take the fourth. Pat, you take the far side. Frenchy you an' yore boys take the near side. I'll go in front across the street from the Algerine, an' Lon an' Jim can take their crowd out in back. Lay low, take no chances an' just keep 'em bottled up. If we handle this right we'll clean 'em out to the last man an' not lose any of our own boys doin' it. Let's go."

After a bit the roofs of the burning buildings caved in

and the walls toppled after. This brought a new burst of ruddy flame that leaped high for a while, but it was soon over. Where the jail and office had stood, there remained areas of blackened embers and graying ash with a few thin columns of smoke curling slowly upwards.

Cole watched the Algerine anxiously and, as a slow hour ticked away without a sign of movement or a sound of any kind coming from the place, he began to sense that all was not well.

Mig Almada came stealing up through the night. "I located Doc McCool," he reported. "He ees over at the store."

"Good," nodded Cole. "Tell me, Mig, are there as many hosses in front of the Algerine now as there were before this trouble started?"

Mig looked the situation over with knitted brows. "Eet ees hard, Señor Cole. I did not really notice much before. Yet, eef I must give answer, I would say there ees not as many."

Premonition began to stir in Cole, a mounting realization that somehow or other he and his men had been tricked. He swore softly. "Damn it all. I got a hunch that crowd have outguessed us, Mig. Me, I'm going up to the Algerine an' have a look."

Even as he made this decision, a shadowy figure came hurrying up. "Hey, Bridger," sounded Lon Sheer's soft, Texan drawl, "things ain't pannin' out right. Out back of the Algerine there's a lot of hoss sign, comin' an' goin'. An' it don't look like there's a soul in the joint. D'yuh think them coyotes could have given us the slip while we was talkin'?"

"That idee was beginnin' to percolate through my thick haid, Lon," answered Cole grimly. "I'm gonna make a sneak an' get a good look inside. I got the feelin' that we're watchin' a empty rat hole."

"C'mon," said Lon quietly. "We'll take that look together."

Without another word Cole led the way up the street some distance, then crossed over and slipped carefully down through the shadows to the Algerine. Lon Sheer kept close at his heels. They reached the corner of the Algerine to move noiselessly along the front of it, until they were crouched just outside the swinging doors.

Cole listened a moment, but not the slightest sound rewarded him. With sudden decision he drew his gun, swung back the doors and stepped through.

His swiftly probing glance showed that his surmise was true. The Algerine was deserted, except for the sprawling bodies of two men, evidently wounded men who had been dragged inside by their comrades and left to die.

Tight-lipped with chagrin and anger, Cole turned to Lon. "Take a glance around upstairs, Lon," he snapped, "I'll see if anyone is in the back rooms."

A moment later Lon came rattling down the stairs to meet Cole just as the latter came back from a fruitless search. "Not a soul," reported Lon. "Anybody out back?"

Cole shook his head. "Plumb empty. Now where an' why did them jaspers leave?"

The front doors swung back with a bang and Mig Almada came leaping through. "Señor Cole—Señor Cole, come quickly! There ees a fire to the south. Eet looks like eet might be the Half Diamond R Ranch," Mig gasped.

They ran outside and looked to the south. Sure enough, a mounting glare lit the black vault of the sky. Cole immediately guessed its import.

The alarm spread quickly. Punchers leaped out of the shadows and raced toward their horses. "Ryan— Frenchy," yelled Cole. "Take half yore men and go guard yore own ranches. The rest of us ride in one crowd. We gotta corner them snakes an' wipe 'em out. No time to waste—make it fast."

The division of forces was soon accomplished and the night was split with the muffled thunder of madly running horses. Clouds of dust arose, swirled sluggishly and settled once more. Presently the pound of hoofs died away, leaving the town in silence. It seemed a town of the dead, the only sign of habitation being in Hoskins' store.

There came a slinking, cautious movement from beneath the raised board sidewalk in front of the Algerine. A man crept forth—a spidery, thin-limbed individual, whose black eyes gleamed in sardonic triumph.

"Suckers," he snarled contemptuously. "A lot of fool suckers—an' that Bridger jasper is the biggest one of the lot. I could hardly keep from pluggin' him when he was standin' right there in front of me. It ain't like Mogy Evans to pass up a chance for revenge like that, but I'll get him later. I reckon Partridge is right. Things will work out better this way."

With this conclusion he slipped back through the shadows and beyond the confines of town. A little way into the brush he came upon a saddled horse, which he mounted and reined away, heading for the crest of a rather lofty hog-backed ridge a couple of miles to the north.

"About an hour before daylight," he muttered. "Things are workin' like a charm."

He rolled and lit a cigarette, then crouched down on his heels, immobile and patient as an Indian.

IX

LONG BEFORE HE AND HIS MADLY RIDING COMPANIONS reached the Half Diamond R Ranch, Cole knew that they were going to be too late to do any good. The glow had risen to its peak and then begun to fade.

At the forks of the trail Cole halted long enough to send Mig Almada and three other men to his own Fish-hook spread to guard against a like occurrence there. Then he swept on with the rest to the Half Diamond R.

Lon Sheer and Jim Early cursed with slow, terrible emphasis as the panting, sweating horses were pulled up at the edge of several masses of glowing embers, where once had stood the Half Diamond R Ranch buildings. All was gone, not even the most humble shed left standing. Even the corrals were gone, with but one or two posts, still licked with sullen flame, left to show where the inclosures had stood.

One of the riders shouted a gruesome discovery. Swinging to and fro on a tightly stretched piece of rope, one end of which was tied to a branch of a nearby cottonwood tree, was a limp, human form. Jim Early and Lon Sheer dashed forward and again the thick, terrible cursing dripped from their lips as they gently cut down the dead body of a weazened little Chinaman.

"Pore ole Ling," rasped Lon hoarsely. "The kindest, friendliest, whitest little Chink I ever knew. An' they dragged him from his kitchen an' lynched him—him who never did anybody a harm or hurt in any way. Damn their black, murderin' souls! They'll pay an' pay plenty for this."

Cole was catechising himself mercilessly. He felt that he should have foreseen something like this and guarded against it. The old homestead of Bill Raine, and of Norma—here he knew a sharper pang—was gone, wiped out by incendiarism. A gentle, defenseless little Chinese cook had been murdered. Cole felt that had he thought faster, all this might have been avoided.

A feeling of futility tore at him, and with that feeling came a tinge of panic. Where next would the swift-riding fiends strike? They seemed as elusive as shadows. Continually Cole's gaze rimmed the entire horizon, watching for another of those telltale glows.

But Cole's true courage and resourcefulness soon reasserted itself. There was nothing further they could do here. "Some of yuh fellers circle around an' see if yuh can pick up the sign that'll show which way they headed from here," he ordered.

The trail was soon ferreted out. It headed directly west across the Punchbowl Hills toward the Fishhook spread. At this discovery the grimness about Cole's eyes deepened. Without a word he sent his bronco racing off on this new trail of vengeance. The punchers pounded along behind him, silent but cold with bitter anger—an anger that would not be appeased until either they or the last man of the brutal raiders was dead.

It was heavy going through the Punchbowl Hills, for though the ridges were not very high, they were criss-crossed with ravine and gulch, arroyo and dry wash, with matted thickets of brush everywhere. The range-bred and trained broncos were put to their utmost cleverness to hold their feet and pace. But they came through finally with triumphant snorts and flattened out with eagerness for the final lap of the race against time.

Abruptly Cole's head jerked up. Above the thunder of hoofs behind him he picked out the faint, whip-like crack of a rifle, coming from the direction of his ranch. It was answered by other reports. A yell or two reached him, thin and far away.

Cole waved his men on. "We're in time," he shouted. "Mig an' the other boys musta made it."

But when Cole reached a point where he could see the ranch buildings, he found that it was not Mig and the others he had sent who were putting up the defense. It was a lone rifleman who seemed to be flitting about the place like a ghost, sending lancing flames and whimpering lead singing through the darkness from many different angles.

Cole halted his men. A bull-like bellow of wrath carried through the night from the ranch buildings. "Come an' get it, yuh sneakin' scoundrels," bawled the heavy voice. "Yuh picked the wrong time to raid this ranch. I may be a ole broken-down cook, but I can still sling lead with the best of 'em. Come an' get it, I say."

This challenge was punctuated with another rattle of rifle fire, some of the lead evidently finding a billet, for a hoarse voice gave a yell of pain and the return fire doubled in intensity.

Cole's eyes gleamed with pride as he turned to Lon Sheer and Jim Early who were riding on either side of him. "That's Oofty Olds," he exclaimed. "Oofty Olds, my cook. Good ole Oofty—doin' his stuff like the fighting grizzly that he is."

Cole twisted in his saddle. "We're chargin' straight in, boys," he told them. "Oofty Olds has held them off so far an' they'll be concentratin' on gettin' him. We'll hit 'em from in back an' hit 'em hard. That must be Mig an' the other boys on the regular trail now. Between us we'll have 'em cornered. Let's ride."

With the bitter memories of the night to spur them, the men needed no second invitation. They spread out in a wide, converging half circle and swept down upon the ranch buildings like an ominous storm. By the time the raiders realized that retribution had caught up with them they were fully inside that arc of vengeance. Then the world became a riot of battle.

Mounted men, cursing and yelling, charged that circle in an attempt to break through. But the flame of gunfire seared their faces and lead cut through their ranks, beating down men and horses alike in a mad tangle of death. The cornered raiders were quick to realize that they were not now battling for a chance to further their night's work of murder and destruction, but were battling for their very lives.

Riding three abreast, Cole and Lon Sheer and Jim Early drove into the battle with cold, surging exultation—the exultation of men at last able to vindicate their wrongs. Lead whispered about them. In back of Cole one of the faithful punchers gave a choking cry and slid headlong to the ground.

Cole's bronco reared and gave an almost human scream, shaking its head violently. As he leaned forward and patted its neck to quiet the brute he felt the warm, wetness of blood, welling from a bullet slash along the sweating hide.

Lon Sheer and Jim Early were living up to their reputation of deadliness. Cole saw Lon send three dim shapes catapulting into eternity with three, cool, carefully placed shots. As for Cole himself, a certain mission obsessed him. He was hunting for Jay Partridge. Partridge was the man he wanted and he spurred his mount from place to place, wherever the fight seemed to be piling up.

In these places he hoped to locate the black-hearted renegade who had thrown the Punchbowl Hills range into this inferno of flame and blood. Cole felt that nothing would satisfy him but to see Partridge on the ground at his feet, gasping out his life before Cole's own smoking guns.

But the search seemed fruitless and the raiders were scattering more with every passing moment. They fled in every direction to escape, dashing around corrals and between the ranch buildings, seeking the open country beyond, toward Mustard Flats. The fight dwindled on Cole's side of the place, but reopened on the far side. Mig and the other boys had arrived.

Now indeed did the raiders go to pieces. Caught between converging lead, they went wild with anger and fear. It became every man for himself and they scattered in all directions, making little attempt to fight back—concentrating everything on escape alone.

From pillar to post through the wild moments they were harried, suffering devastating losses before the remnants of their band finally broke through to partial safety. Abruptly the tumult ceased and the victorious punchers began taking stock.

Under Cole's directions they dismounted and went about through a swiftly graying dawn, identifying the dead and wounded. Cole's band had lost three men, the riders nine. But none of those nine was Jay Partridge or

Flash Condon. The real culprits had again eluded retribution, it seemed.

Cole was disconcerted. As long as these two were free the big job of cleaning up was unfinished. He looked about him through the rapidly approaching day. As his eyes scanned the horizon they suddenly came to rest once more upon that dread omen—smoke! But this time that smoke rose in two slim, straight columns, so evenly spaced and so dense that they seemed to bear a special significance.

The smoke lay far to the northeast, somewhere about the town of Baird or beyond. Cole called Lon and Jim to him and pointed out those two distant, pillar-like columns. Even as the two Texans looked, one of those columns broke into ragged, measured blobs, lazily climbing and fanning away. The column steadied into solidity again and the other one was broken up.

Lon reached for his bridle rein. "That's sign talk," he drawled. "Somebody is sendin' a message to somebody else. It ain't for us, so it must be for Partridge and Condon, wherever they are. What it means, I dunno; but it means somethin'."

"There's just one place now that ain't too well guarded," suggested Jim Early.

"An' that is town," broke in Cole. "I'll bet that's it, boys. We cain't gamble no more; we gotta be shore. I'll leave Mig an' enough of the boys here to see that the raiders don't come back an' clean up. The rest of us sand it for town. Make it fast."

They made it fast, but even as they spurred their

weary broncos away on this new lead, Jay Partridge, Flash Condon and a round dozen of their renegade riders were slipping like shadows across the flats toward town from the west. They had hidden out there while sending the balance of their gang to raid the Half Diamond R and the Fishhook ranches.

By the time Cole and his men were half a mile from the Fishhook Ranch, Partridge was leading his crowd into the southern end of the main street of Baird. His objective was Hoskins' store, where wounded men groaned in unconsciousness and where Norma Raine, white and weary of face, was crouched beside her father, sleeping fitfully with her head upon his knee.

X

It had been a hard night in the store for all concerned. Doc McCool, a tall, lank, rather sad-faced man, had not closed an eye all through the long, hard, dreary hours. He had managed to do a fair job of setting Red Kester's broken shoulder. Then he gave the tortured Red an opiate that sent the big, flaming-haired puncher off into a fitful sleep.

But the doctor's biggest concern was Spud Merrick. Spud was in a bad way, a very bad way. When Norma, who had helped the doctor as well as she could, asked a low-voiced query about Spud's chances, Doc McCool had shaken his head.

"He's got a chance—a slim one, Miss Raine. It all

depends on my being able to find that slug and get it out of him. If I can and no untoward complications set in, he may pull through. If I don't get the lead—well—" The doctor shrugged.

After a tense half hour that left Norma limp and haggard, the doctor had recovered the slug. Spud was very weak when the job was finished, but he had the vitality to hang on and he passed the midnight hours safely with signs of returning strength. But Doc McCool never left Spud's side, hovering over him constantly.

When Cole had led his men on that mad dash out of town at sight of the glow which had meant the burning of the Half Diamond R Ranch, Norma had questioned her father as to what the reason was. Bill Raine did not know but sent Foxy Billings and Sad Samson outside to try and gather some reason for the move.

Foxy and Sad were not long in drawing correct conclusions. When they told Raine, the only sign of how the loss struck him was in the tightening of his lips and the chilling glitter in his deep-set eyes.

"Don't spread the news," he muttered tersely. "No use makin' Norma feel any worse about things than she does already. The pore kid is about worried to a rag as it is."

To Norma's questioning later, Raine shrugged. "Partridge an' his gang musta flew the coop, honey. Cole's after him, tooth an' nail. That boy'll make this a white man's country before he gets through."

Tired as she was, Norma managed a tremulous smile at this. She held her own delicious secret—the memory of Cole's lips still burning warm upon her own. It glorified her to see the outspoken confidence her father felt in Cole Bridger.

It was hard for Bill Raine to remain in the store while harried by the knowledge that his ranch was being razed by Partridge and the other renegades. Every fiber of his belligerent old body cried out for action—direct flaming action against those despoilers of the range country.

But Raine was sensible enough to realize that one member, more or less added to or taken away from Cole's band, would not change the complexion of things. Besides, there was Norma to consider and safeguard. It was not beyond the realm of possibility that Partridge might sneak back on the nearly defenseless town again. Raine realized that in such event, his place would be beside his daughter.

Norma had told him of the initial attempt to kidnap her and of her escape. Her father knew that Partridge would not hesitate to carry her off again if the opportunity offered, for this would give him a hold over Raine equal to nothing else.

The night wore away. Towards dawn, Norma crept up to her father's side and put her head on his knee. In this manner she fell asleep, while Raine's gnarled, old hand caressed her hair with infinite gentleness.

Foxy and Sad had been taking turns at keeping guard and it was Sad who was on post when daylight came. He stepped outside for a smoke and a chance to stretch his muscles. The town lay ominously quiet and somehow Sad sensed a hovering threat in the air. He began cautiously patrolling the street, alert and watchful. Where the jail and the sheriff's office had stood was now merely a ragged patch of charred wood.

There were three sprawled figures in sight also, lying stiff and grotesque in the dust of the single street. Sad was just considering the advisability of dragging from sight these grim reminders of the savage night before, when some premonition caused him to whirl and look along the street. There, just moving into sight, came a group of horsemen. Sad recognized Partridge and Flash Condon in the lead.

With a hoarse yell of warning for those in the store, Sad raced for the shelter of the doorway, dragging out his six-gun as he went. Flash Condon was the first of the raiders to catch the significance of Sad's actions. He sank home the spurs and sent his horse lunging down the street, in a wild attempt to head Sad off. As he came Condon whipped out his gun and began to shoot.

Bullets whimpered about Sad, plucking at his clothes, kicking up gouts of dust about his flying feet. Sad slammed back lead in return and a chance slug from his gun took Condon's mount through the head.

The racing horse stumbled, lurched and turned completely over, hurling its rider from the saddle. Condon ploughed through the dust of the street, awkward and grotesque. By the time he had recovered his bewildered senses, Sad had gained the doorway of the store.

It was now Condon's turn for precipitate retreat and

he lost no time in making it, with the charge of Partridge and the other renegades to cover him. But that charge soon broke. At the sound of the racket, Foxy Billings was out of his sleep and at Sad's side in two jumps.

He carried a Winchester carbine in his hands. Before Partridge and his men could wheel back and put a building between themselves and the store, Foxy had neatly emptied two saddles. Sad added another casualty with his six-gun, swearing wildly because it seemed that the running Condon bore a charmed life. Sad did his best to pick off the outlaw leader, but without success.

The shooting of Sad and Foxy had one good effect, however. It caused sufficient pause on the part of the renegades to allow those in the store to make ready a defense. Everyone, except the two wounded men, was immediately alive to the gravity of the situation. Of able-bodied defenders, there were but five—Foxy, Sad, Bill Raine, Ezra Hoskins and Doc McCool.

But fighting was not McCool's profession. He soon showed that he would be of little use, except in aiding Norma to reload the rifles and revolvers for the others.

Dried-up, twangy-voiced Hoskins unearthed a sawed-off shotgun of awesome bore and took a grim-eyed position at one of the front windows. Bill Raine took the other window, while Sad and Foxy, from behind a barricade of flour and grain sacks, commanded the door.

When Norma stole up to her father's side he turned

on her grimly. "Yuh gotta keep back, child," he told her. "This is a man's work. Oh, I know yuh can shoot as well as most men, but I cain't have yuh takin' the risk. If yuh don't get back outa sight I'll go straight out in that street. I swear I will."

Norma obeyed him, knowing that he would do just as he threatened. The attack was not long in materializing. Partridge and Condon well knew that their ruse would not long remain undiscovered. Besides, they had little taste to test strength with Cole Bridger and his men out in the open. This little job had to be done quickly and completely.

Partridge had two objectives in the store; one was Bill Raine, and the other was Norma. During the wild night Partridge had glimpsed Norma. He realized that in some way she had gotten away from the Mexican he had sent to guard her at the cabin back on Table Mountain. A strange madness had gripped Partridge from the moment Norma had faced him so defiantly in the sheriff's office at the time of her visit to Cole Bridger.

Partridge wanted Norma Raine and was determined to have her. Not only were purely selfish personal ideas concerned there, but he realized that things were going none too smooth in his scheme for power. He was aware that with Norma as his prisoner he would hold a hostage for whom he could demand almost any terms he wished.

"Make it fast," he told his men harshly. "Spread out and come in on them from all sides. I don't care what happens to anyone else in that store, but whatever yuh do, kill Bill Raine and get the girl. But I want her unharmed in any way; don't forget that."

Again the harassed town of Baird became a battle-field. In accordance with Partridge's order, the renegades sought various posts of vantage and cover; they soon began to pour a heavy fire upon the store with rifle and six-gun. Inside, the air was full of flying splinters and whimpering lead. But the defenders were all crouched close to the floor with barricades of merchandise to shield them, and for some time little harm was done.

When Partridge figured that the furious fire directed upon the store had sufficiently cowed the defenders, he signaled for a rush. It was a costly move. The moment his men charged into the open, they were met by a blare of gunfire that beat them back in a broken wave.

Ezra Hoskins' shotgun boomed heavily and scattered a hail of buckshot that bit and stung like a hive of hornets. The distance was a little long for any real effectiveness by the shotgun, but the moral force was great. The raiders had little stomach for facing that bellowing demon at a range close enough for the buckshot to bite really deep.

The deadly work was done by Foxy and Sad, who improved each shining moment with deliberate accuracy. Bill Raine got in one good try; but he was half blinded by a cloud of splinters the next moment, as a slug tore through the window-sill not a foot from his head.

The rush broke and receded, leaving several stark forms upon the street. Partridge was literally blazing with rage. Flash Condon was even more angry. He turned on Partridge, snarling like a wolf.

"Enough of that foolishness," he snapped. "If yuh're callin' for any more suicide stunts like that—yuh lead the parade, savvy? I ain't gonna stand for my men bein' slaughtered like that again. I'm in this with yuh to a finish, but from now on I wanta see some haid-work. Otherwise I take over the whip myself."

Partridge's eyes filmed with anger, but he had sense enough to realize that it would never do to quarrel with Condon and thus run a chance of losing the outlaw chief's support at this time. "We'll try the rear of the place," he growled. "Have some of the boys keep 'em busy here in front. The rest of us go out back."

But even as they began marking out a division of men, a single spidery, slinking figure stole softly up to the rear door of the store and, finding that portal securely bolted, tried a window which was not locked. Smoothly as a weasel on the hunt, the fellow crept inside and, with drawn guns, moved on into the big front room where the defenders were grouped.

It was Doc McCool who saw Mogy Evans first. He started to shout a warning, but Evans was on him like a panther, his gun lifting and falling in a vicious arc. The heavy barrel of the weapon crunched home on McCool's head and the doctor slumped limply to the floor.

"Raine," barked Evans, "I'm after yuh. Claude couldn't do it, but I can. Yuh were the cause of him bein' killed."

At the sound of the thin, venomous voice, Bill Raine whirled and lunged partially erect. Instinctively he ducked his head. It was well that he did so, for Evans had shot deliberately at the center of Raine's face. Raine's movement caused the slug to strike high, ripping along his scalp and flinging him stunned and bleeding under the window he had guarded.

Norma, seeing her father go down, screamed and ran for him, unwittingly crossing the line of sight Ezra Hoskins was drawing on Evans with his shotgun. Forced to hold his fire for the fractional second which gave Evans the edge, Hoskins felt a terrific impact at the breech of his shotgun—a blow that shattered his right hand with splattering lead and which knocked the weapon from his grasp.

Foxy and Sad were caught cold. Evans' next shot tore through Foxy's right shoulder, piling him up in a heap. Sad had little better luck. He got off a shot that ripped along Evans' ribs, but took a slug through the chest in reply. Sad slumped forward slowly, his hands gripping at the wound.

Casually punching the empty shells from his gun, Evans advanced up the room. In the sudden silence which had fallen there was only one sound. Norma, her father's bloody head clasped in her arms, was sobbing softly and murmuring broken endearments. Ezra Hoskins stared first at his shattered hand and then at

Evans, with the look of a man hardly able to believe his senses.

A narrow, sardonic sneer twisted Evans' lips. He felt supremely satisfied with himself. The way Bill Raine had dropped convinced Evans that his shot had gone true—straight through old Raine's head.

Of the others he had shot down, Evans gave not the slightest thought. They were incidentals. Half of a vow he had made was performed. He had shot Bill Raine down. There remained another to feel the bite of his lead before that vow was fulfilled. Cole Bridger was to be the next.

Outside, startled and wondering at the sudden fusillade which had taken place in the store, the raiders were holding their fire and waiting to see what would develop. They were amazed to recognize Mogy Evans as he swaggered from the doorway of the store and lifted his hand in careless greeting.

Jay Partridge sprang from his place of concealment and crossed the street. "What happened in there?" he demanded.

Evans shrugged. "I came in the back way an' sorta cleaned up. Hit McCool over the haid with my gun, smashed Hoskins' hand an' rocked off Raine an' them two Fishhook punchers, Foxy an' Sad. Yore crowd can make more fuss an' get less results than any outfit I ever saw. Now for Bridger, damn his soul! He's next on my list."

Partridge heard the callous, cold-blooded boasting of Evans with intense satisfaction. "Is the girl all right?" he asked anxiously.

Evans grunted. "Far as I know. She's in there weepin' an' wailin'. Don't know how she got away from Pancho. I left her at that ole cabin with him. She tricked him some way. What d'yuh want her for now?"

"My business," said Partridge curtly. "C'mon, we'll go in an' get her."

They went back into the store and found valiant little Ezra Hoskins doing his pitiful best to handle a Winchester with one hand. Evans, quick as a leaping wolf, was on the storekeeper with a curse, hurling the rifle to one side with one hand, while with the other he swung a brutal blow to Hoskins' jaw. The storekeeper went down and was still.

Norma was working over her father when Partridge caught her by the shoulder, pulling her away. She whirled on him like a tigress at bay, her eyes flaming.

"You beast—you murdering dog—don't you touch me!" she flared.

Partridge laughed exultantly and tightened his grip. "Easy does it," he mocked. "Come along quietly and you won't be mishandled. If you try and fight it will be the worse for you. . . . Evans, are you sure Raine is dead?"

The viperish little gunman's ego was affronted by this remark. "Don't he look it?" he rasped. "I don't miss 'em at that range. Of course he's daid."

At this moment Flash Condon stuck his head in the doorway. "Make it fast," he growled. "There's dust

135

showin' along the Fishhook trail. Riders comin'. Let's get out to Orcutt's place while the goin' is good."

"Maybe it's our boys," suggested Partridge hopefully.

"Yeah, an' maybe it ain't," retorted Condon. "Me, I've come to the point where I figger it's about time to start playin' safe. Yuh don't want to make the mistake of misjudgin' the other feller all the time, Partridge. We fooled Bridger once, but don't go reckonin' too strong that he's gonna fall for that stuff all the time. I say let's ride, while the ridin' is good."

"Okeh," conceded Partridge. "Orcutt's it is. Hack won't like it, but he's been tryin' to straddle the fence too long. He's either with us or against us to a final finish. . . . C'mon, Mogy, give me a hand with this girl."

Norma, dazed and despairing, fought mechanically. But her strength was of little avail against the combined efforts of the two men. She was half dragged, half carried from the store and tied to the saddle of a horse, the rider of which had been killed in the initial rush upon the store.

The girl's mind was a bedlam of nightmare and terror. She believed, as Evans had stated, that her father was dead. That sinister belief pounded and pounded at her until it seemed her mind would break before the impact. And when the bonds were tightened that held her to the saddle she slumped, half unconscious over the bronco's neck.

At a sweeping gallop the raiders headed out of town,

taking the northwest trail towards Hack Orcutt's H Bar O Connected Ranch.

In the store there was the sound of movement. There came groans and scuffling. Then Doc McCool, a smear of crimson down the side of his thin face, struggled to his feet.

A long, slow glance brought home the situation to him. He shook his head, mopped the blood from his face, and began, with professional skill, to examine the injuries of the various huddled figures on the floor. He was well into this task when Cole Bridger, at the head of his men, galloped into town.

XI

A GLANCE AT THE SPRAWLED FIGURES OF THE DEAD raiders in the street, gave Cole an inkling of what to expect. As he plunged through the doorway of the store his face was white and bleak, his eyes tortured.

"Norma," he called. "Norma! Where are yuh?"

Doc McCool's uplifted hand stilled Cole's shouts. In the stunned silence that came over Cole and Lon and Jim Early, who had pressed in with Cole, the doctor explained in a monotone.

"Partridge and the rest have Miss Raine. They are taking her out to Hack Orcutt's ranch. It was Mogy Evans who enabled them to do it. We were standing Partridge and those devils of his off successfully when Evans sneaked in a back way. I saw him first, but before I could do a thing he hit me over the head with his gun, knocking me out momentarily.

"I don't know how he shot down all these others, but he did it. I was just coming to when Evans and Partridge were taking Miss Raine away. She was unharmed. I heard them say they were taking her to Orcutt's place. As soon as they were gone I got to work."

"The boss—Bill Raine—is he daid?" asked Lon Sheer thickly.

"No; he got an awful nasty wallop, but the bullet went high. I don't think he has concussion. He seems to be coming along strongly. Sad Samson is dead, and Foxy Billings has got a smashed shoulder. Hoskins got a torn hand and a slam on the jaw, but he's doing fine."

"Yuh're—yuh're shore Norma wasn't hurt, Doc?" protested Cole.

"I didn't see everything, of course," answered McCool; "me being knocked as cold as a mackerel. But I assume she was all right. She gave those rascals quite a battle before they got her out of here. I'd say there was nothing wrong with her."

Cole turned and started for the door. Jim Early noted the expression on his face and caught him by the arm.

"Take it slow, Bridger," he drawled kindly. "I know just how yuh feel, but yuh cain't ride right into the middle of that rattlesnake nest an' get away with it. I don't think we got to worry much about Miss Norma—not just yet, anyhow.

"I think I got the idea why Partridge ran off with her;

138

he realizes now that in open fight we got him licked. He'll probably make a last stand at Orcutt's an' if it don't pan out he'll use Miss Norma as a hostage. He'll try an' make us pay one way or another for her safety. Let's get organized again."

Cole was quick to see the wisdom of Jim Early's advice. Though his whole being was inflamed with but one idea, and that was to storm through to Norma's side regardless of risk or cost, he got sufficient grip upon himself to move more circumspectly. He detailed two men from his already depleted band to stay at the store and help Doc McCool.

"I don't reckon we need to worry about defendin' the store against Partridge again," he concluded. "They got what they came after an' they'll steer clear of town for a while now. There's nine of us left. We'll be out-numbered at the H Bar O Connected, but the way I feel, I don't care if there's a hundred of 'em to tangle with. How about it, Lon—an' you, Jim?"

"So far," drawled Lon slowly, his gaze upon Bill Raine's white face, "so far Jim an' me ain't had much chance to do our stuff. When we hit that ranch we'll show them fellers how we used to do things down in the Panhandle, eh, Jim?"

"Correct," nodded Jim. "We got enough men, Bridger, so we might as well start."

Cole delayed only long enough to distribute more ammunition among his men from the shelves of the store, then flung himself into his saddle and led the way out the northwest trail. He well knew the necessity of keeping his head now, with what appeared to be the final crisis coming up. But it was a stiff battle between reasoning power and utter, animal fury.

The consciousness that he loved Norma Raine, had been growing upon Cole for several days—from that very first moment of introduction in the store, in fact. Somehow, at the first glance, her charm, her freshness, her wholesome beauty had stirred him.

When he had brushed that swift kiss upon her lips in the store after escaping from the burning jail, there had been a hint of emotional impulsiveness behind the act. Yet there was something else besides this same deepening consciousness of feeling that he had not been able to qualify fully, but which he realized was powerful and sweeping beyond any he had ever experienced before.

It was when he looked at that blood-stained, bullet-riddled store just now, that he really understood what Norma Raine meant to him. The first fear that he might find her huddled lifeless, was torture beyond all description. The true knowledge of what had transpired changed this fear to a gnawing, white-hot fury that shook him like a storm.

All of the natural amiability of his make-up was gone. His lips were a tense, thin line; his eyes pools of narrow-lidded ice. He rode with a singleness of purpose that carried him ahead of the men following, like a racing wolf.

And besides Norma's predicament, he had the memory of Sad Samson to feed the anger which harried him—good, hard-working old Sad. Nicknamed by cowboy humor at exact opposites to what his real nature was.

Sad had been the cheeriest, jolliest puncher imaginable. He had always been friendly, always smiling, always unselfishly ready to do a favor or good turn for anyone, anywhere. But Sad was dead now, cut down by the lead of a slinking, twisted-mouth killer whose penchant was shooting men in the back.

Cole was swayed by the strange impression that the world had turned darker; that the sun had lost much of its brightness; that he was riding through mocking shadows. He had killed several men during his lifetime.

In all of these cases it had been a matter of self-defense and entirely justified. And, though these victims had in every case been renegades whose passing was a benefit to society at large, after nearly every fatal clash Cole had secretly deplored the necessity of blood-letting.

There was no such regret touching him now. He felt that the greatest satisfaction in life would be to see Partridge, Mogy Evans, and Flash Condon crumple and die before his smoking guns. He was wildly impatient for the opportunity of meeting them in a final showdown, and hungry for the sight of them lying huddled and still before him. Cole Bridger had turned killer with a vengeance.

Riding in the forefront of the others, Lon Sheer and Jim Early were readily cognizant of Cole's black, killing, reckless mood.

"We'll have to watch him, Jim," said Lon, nodding at Cole. "The way he feels now he'll bust into that combine liked a locoed steer. We gotta keep an eye on him. Way I figger it, it won't do Miss Norma much good if we get her out safe an' sound an' Bridger stops some lead. It's a natural, between them two."

"My sentiments exactly, Lon," nodded Early. "Let's get up alongside him, so when we reach the H Bar O Connected he won't go bargin' in, regardless."

The two Texans urged their weary mounts to greater speed and drew up beside Cole. He did not look at them. His gaze was straight ahead, set and grim. There was something almost awesome in his singleness of purpose.

Jim Early looked down at the trail as it unwound before them. "They ain't far ahead of us," he announced. "There's new-turned dust that ain't had time to bleach yet."

Lon nodded. Cole did not seem to hear at all. Lon pushed his mount close against Cole's.

"Shake that mood, son," he said quietly. "Yuh're gonna kill yore hoss an' yoreself, too, if yuh don't take a hitch on yore feelin's. Now don't try an' clean up single-handed. I got an idee how yuh feel, but yuh wanta keep the ole haid workin' all the time. If yuh don't yuh'll shore get yoreself scragged. An' that won't help nobody, especially Miss Norma."

Cole heard Lon's words dimly, as though feebly battling against the malignant cloak which enfolded him.

He caught at them, considered them, and became more rational. He slowed his mount slightly and drew a big breath.

"Yuh're right," he panted hoarsely. "Thanks, Lon. I reckon I was plumb loco."

They swept around the northern end of the Punchbowl Hills and the ranch buildings of the H Bar O Connected were in sight. A group of men had just dismounted before the place. One of them immediately caught sight of Cole and his band. He had evidently shouted an alarm, for the dismounted renegades scattered quickly, some to the main house, others through the outer buildings of the ranch.

Immediately came the faint, far-off snapping of rifle fire and gusts of dust were kicked up a hundred yards or more away. Cole reined in and let his men gather around him. For a time he was silent. Then he looked slowly over his followers.

"It ain't gonna be easy," he said jerkily, nodding toward the ranch. "We'll have to eat lead a-plenty before we collect. I ain't askin' any man to risk his life for his hire. This is mainly my battle an' Bill Raine's. I won't think any the less of anybody who figgers now is a good time to draw out."

"Shut up an' talk sense, yuh buffle-haided chump," growled Whip O'Conner, from the edge of the crowd. "I ain't had so much fun since I found a rattlesnake in my bed. We're all ridin' this thing to a finish—root hawg or die."

Cole nodded soberly. "I just wanted to be shore.

Much obliged for puttin' me right, Whip. We'll have great times together on this range, once we get it purified."

Even with the primal desire to come to immediate hand-grips with Partridge and the others stirring him, Cole now calmed down sufficiently to realize that an attempt to charge the H Bar O Connected ranch buildings in the broad light of day would be worse than suicidal.

Night was the logical time to make the assault, when he and his men would have the protective covering of darkness to work in. He looked over his faithful followers. There were enough of them to throw a thin line of watchers completely about the place. In this way they could see that the renegades did not make another break for freedom which would carry them clear. At the same time, he could do with more men.

"Do yuh think that gang we broke up last night will recover enough to try any more raids on any of the ranches, Lon?" he asked.

Lon grunted and shook his head. "Don't think so, Cole. Yuh see, we know that Partridge, Condon, Orcutt an' Evans are all down yonder at the H Bar O Connected. That crowd we salivated last night are leaderless an' pretty badly shot up. The chances are strong that they've scattered plumb to hell-an'-gone with no more stomach left for raidin' ranches or anythin' else. Not for a time, anyhow.

"I know that breed pretty well. They have to have somebody else to do their thinkin' for 'em, an' they ain't got that person handy just now. If yuh're figgerin' on gettin' Ryan an' Frenchy an' some more men to help out here, I think it's plumb safe to send for 'em."

"Good," nodded Cole. "I was hopin' that. We'd be fools to try an' rush Orcutt's ranch in daylight. But tonight—well, we're goin' after 'em. An' I kinda reckon Pat an' Frenchy would like to be in on the showdown. . . . Whip, yuh ole rannyhan, d'yuh feel like doin' some more ridin'? I know yuh're all in, but I'd like yuh to go."

Whip O'Conner's fiery thatch bristled. "The only time I'm all in is when I cain't crawl, Cole," he answered. "Shore I'll ride. I'm good for a week steady of this sort of stuff."

"Then make a circle an' get Pat an' Frenchy. If they leave a couple of their men to watch the ranches, that ought to be enough. Yuh can hit my spread too, and get Mig to come along with yuh. Leave Oofty an' one other feller to watch the Fishhook, but bring everybody else. Tell the boys not to kill any hosses gettin' here. Long as they arrive by dark it'll be soon enough."

"Bueno," nodded Whip as he reined away. "See yuh later."

As Whip departed, Cole set about sending the remaining members of his band out into a wide circle that completely surrounded the buildings of Orcutt's ranch.

"Don't try an' pull any private feuds, boys," he ordered. "Just lay quiet an' watch. If any of that crowd down there make a try at a getaway, do what yuh can

145

to stop 'em. Soon as we hear the shootin' some of the rest of us will get around to help out. I don't think they'll try that, however.

"Evidently they figger they've got enough men to stand us off till kingdom come. Besides, they've got Miss Raine down there an' may try an' use her as a hostage to make terms with us. Come dark an' the rest of the gang show up, we'll start workin' in close where we can show Partridge that he don't know human nature a-tall. Now scatter an' hold on until further notice."

The punchers rode warily to their posts and in half an hour a thin circle of cold-eyed, hawk-faced men lounged and smoked at ease, but never for one moment relaxed their vigilance.

Not until Partridge ushered Norma Raine into the H Bar O Connected ranch house did the clammy horror of those dreadful moments in the store begin to lift from her mind. She had been like one in a daze, saying nothing, moving listlessly. But with the first shock passing, she regained in some measure her poise and courage.

Her face was white and her eyes haunted. Whenever she looked down and saw the crimson stains on her clothes where her father's head had rested, she shuddered and bit her lips cruelly to keep from crying out.

Hack Orcutt had met Partridge and the other arrivals in the yard, and his heavy, blocky face was sullen and angry. At Partridge's snapping request for a room to hold Norma prisoner, Orcutt had said nothing. He merely led the way to a small room in the east wing of the house. The room was crudely furnished with a blanketed bunk, a chair, and a table upon which lay a dusty pile of dog-eared magazines and stock journals.

The single window was shrouded by a pair of heavy shutters that were drawn and locked on the outside, making the room gloomy with shadows.

"This'll hold her," growled Orcutt sulkily. "Though I don't see what in hell yore idee was in bringin' her here."

Partridge whirled on the treacherous ranchman viciously. "Enough of that kind of talk, Orcutt," he snarled. "You're a bigger frost than I thought you were. You were glad to throw in with us when you first heard our plans. But I can see now that the only inducement you were considering was the chance to rustle your neighbors clean. You thought that you could make a lot of easy money without incurring any risk.

"I can see that you're sore because we came here to make our final stand. A sure-thing gambler is what you are. It was all right for the rest of us to take big chances on getting killed while you sat fat and easy, gleaning all the profits.

"Now that you're called on to show everybody just where you stand and to do your share of the fighting, you're getting ready to squeal. Well, let me tell you one thing. You're in this just as deep as me or Flash or Evans or any of our boys. You'll fight as we fight and when."

Orcutt's beefy face had grown choleric with color at Partridge's words, but he did not answer back. He slunk out and slammed the door behind him. Partridge's lips were set in a sardonic sneer of contempt as he stared at the closed door a moment. Then he turned to Norma, wiping the viciousness from his features and replacing it with what was meant as a conciliatory smile.

"You understand, Miss Raine," he began, his voice oily and unctuous, "that I sincerely regret some of the steps I have had to take since—"

Norma's uplifted hand and blazing eyes silenced him. "I understand many things," she said coldly. "I understand that you are a liar and a crook, a murderer and a coward. I have no wish to hear anything you might say. I despise you to an unbelievable extent. Kindly leave me to myself."

"Very well," he rasped harshly. "Take that attitude if you like. Before I get through with you, you'll sing a different tune."

Norma thought for a moment that he was going to lay hands on her, but an interruption in the form of Flash Condon's voice sounded outside the door.

"They're throwin' a circle of men around the place, Partridge. Yuh better forget the girl for a while an' get out here. I don't like the look of things."

Partridge cursed softly, whirled on his heel and went out. Norma heard the lock of the door snap into place. Slowly she crossed to the bunk and sank down upon it. Her shoulders drooped, her slim hands clenched and unclenched, and she shut her eyes tight. But it was of no use. She could not stop the tears.

When the outburst had passed she straightened up, miraculously calmed and steady of mind.

Cole Bridger would be out there among the faithful—and Lon Sheer and Jim Early. She knew that none of these three would ever rest or stop fighting while her safety was in the balance. Death was all that could halt them.

XII

THERE WAS NO SLEEP FOR COLE BRIDGER, HOWEVER. Cole was gaunt and hollow-eyed and the furrows which bracketed his grim lips were cut deep. But the feverish impatience and activity which gripped him drove all thought of weariness from him.

While waiting for the arrival of reinforcements and the protective blackness of night to start the assault, he rode continuously about the line of watchers. He had scattered several men around the H Bar O Connected Ranch, intent upon seeing that his quarry did not sneak through the lines and elude him again. And these faithful watchers, seeing the look upon Cole's face, redoubled their alertness.

At four in the afternoon Pat Ryan and Frenchy Gaston, with several of their riders, came up. Cole greeted them with quiet sincerity. "Thanks, boys. We got 'em cooped up complete this time. They've gone to burrow like scared coyotes. They hold one edge over us, however. They have Miss Raine captive there at the ranch house. We'll have to watch our lead when we finally cut loose tonight."

"Is that right what Whip told us—that Bill Raine is shot?" asked Pat Ryan.

Cole nodded. "Mogy Evans did it. He crippled Foxy Billings and Ezry Hoskins an' killed pore Sad Samson besides. Sneaked in the back door of the store an' cut 'em down before they knew what had happened. Bill was lucky. Got creased. The doc says he'll come along all right."

At this moment a buckboard hove into view, creaking along behind a fast-stepping pair of broncos, corning from the direction of town. Cole gave vent to an exclamation of astonishment. Mig Almada was driving it, with his saddled horse trotting along behind, empty stirrups swaying and slapping. On the seat beside Mig sat a gaunt, hunched figure, crowned with a cap of white bandages.

When the buckboard came to a rattling stop, Cole looked into the white face and bloodshot eyes of Bill Raine. The old cattleman appeared ready to collapse, but the indomitable will of him rose ascendant over his physical weakness.

"I couldn't help myself, Señor Cole," explained Mig swiftly. "I came through town on my way here an' Beel was out een the street, just trying to get into the seat of hees buckboard. Doc McCool was geeving heem hell, but Beel would not listen. So, as we could not stop heem all I could do was drive for heem and see that he got here."

"Yuh danged peanut-brained ole fool," exclaimed Pat Ryan in candid affection to Raine. "Don't yuh realize that yuh can push yore luck too far? After old Doc McCool pullin' yuh through yuh're out here tryin' to undo all his good work. Yuh'd feel kinda silly if yuh up an' died from complications, wouldn't yuh?"

Raine did not answer. He stared at Cole. "Where's Norma?" he muttered hoarsely.

Cole nodded towards the distant ranch house. "We're goin' after her as soon as it gets dark, Bill," he explained. "We've got men completely surrounding this place. They won't sneak through again on us."

"Mig tells me there ain't a stick of the ole home ranch left standin'," went on Raine. "They burned it just outa pure cussedness."

"I consider that my fault, Bill," said Cole quietly. "I shoulda kept a better watch on the Algerine. That was greenhorn stuff to let 'em slip out like they did."

Raine waved an admonishing hand. "Not yore fault. We all been playin' the sucker for Partridge. I'm stickin' here until the finish."

They helped him from the buckboard and spread a blanket for him to lie on, with another stretched as a sun-break. Mig Almada had thoughtfully heaped the back of the buckboard with a supply of canned food-stuffs and a small keg of water. He set about busily distributing the food and drink to the watchers.

During all this time the ranch lay quiet, ominously

so. Cole knew that down there preparations were being made to repel the attack he planned. But he shrugged grimly at his conclusions. Let them make their preparations; he was making preparations also.

The sun dipped into the west, seeming to pause a moment in a bath of fluid gold, before dipping finally from sight. Purple shadows lengthened and grew; mists arose to cloud the world; a cooling breeze sprang up. Far in the distance a coyote yapped forlornly at the first stars.

Cole, who had downed a bite of food at Mig Almada's thoughtful insistence, rolled a cigarette, settled his gunbelt about his hips and picked up the reins of his horse. The time for action had arrived. He turned to Pat Ryan, Frenchy Gaston, Lon and Jim and Mig and one or two others he had kept with him to receive final instructions.

"Mig," he ordered, "ride the circle and tell the boys to start closin' in. Tell 'em to work slow. We got all night. Tell 'em not to break the circle under any conditions an' to keep in touch with the men on either side of 'em.

"Pat, yuh an' Frenchy keep workin' back an' forth, sorta overseein' things. Lon an' Jim an' me are goin' to tackle the place in front and keep pushin' straight through until we break in. An' pass around the word that there ain't no use in botherin' with prisoners. Those jaspers started this. We'll finish it for 'em."

As the men mounted and rode away on their appointed tasks, Bill Raine called Cole to him. "Son," he said, rising upon one elbow, "yuh know what I'm livin' for. Damn the home ranch bein' burned an' all that. All I'm thinkin' about now is Norma. Yuh'll bring her out safe to me—won't yuh, lad?"

The old fellow's voice shook as he voiced this request. Cole gripped his hand. "I'll bring her out safe or I won't come out myself, Bill," he replied simply. "Now yuh just take it easy an' don't worry. I expect Mig will be keepin' an eye on yuh. *Adios*."

Cole swung into his saddle and, with Lon and Jim beside him, began moving slowly down the long slope towards the buildings, lying dark and still. Suddenly he felt quieted, calmly certain of himself. The nervous suspense of waiting was over. Direct action lay before him and such action was the only thing which could bring satisfaction to the burning impatience which swayed him.

Cole and the two Texans approached within two hundred yards of the ranch before some eagle-eyed defender picked out the movement of them through the rapidly thickening darkness. A rifle spanged sharply and a bullet whimpered by overhead.

"Far enough for a time," drawled Cole quietly, swinging to the ground. "I was hopin' we could make it to this little swale. We can leave the hosses here an' go on afoot."

Dismounted, both riders and mounts were safe from flying lead in the little hollow Cole had headed for. It was well that they were below the line of fire, for a nervous volley crashed out on the heels of that first shot,

153

filling the air with sibilant hissing. Waiting a moment for the shooting to stop, the three men worked up carefully from the low swale and started a slow advance upon the ranch buildings.

They did not hurry. As Cole had told Mig Almada, they had all night and nothing would be gained by a premature attack. Cole's idea was a gradual tightening of the net he had thrown about the place, a steadily growing pressure that would be liable to unsettle the defenders and cause them to break in confusion.

So far, not a shot had been fired for hours by any of Cole's men, a fact which gratified him very much. No careless, wild-shooting punchers, were these working with him. Instead, they were a cold-eyed, iron-nerved bunch of riders grimly intent on stamping upon the head of this poisonous plot to wreck the Punchbowl Hills range. When the time came to shoot, they would throw lead with a vengeance and in a way that meant something.

As the darkness settled down, black and velvety, Cole and Lon and Jim renewed their advance. They moved in a crouch, well bent over, for they knew the penchant nervous men had for shooting high in the dark. The ranch was silent once more. Fifty yards from the buildings, Cole called another halt, dropping flat on his stomach. Lon and Jim inched up on either side of him.

"I'd shore like to know just what part of the house they got Miss Norma in," he murmured. "I'm leery of shootin' until I know where she is. Tell yuh what, boys—I'm goin' on ahead an' try an' locate her. Give me five minutes' start, then roll a gunful of lead towards the corrals.

"Soon as yuh do, duck an' move off to one side. The shootin' will draw their attention to this spot an' give me a chance to work right along the edge of the house. There's just a chance that I might get her out without them knowin' it. It's worth the try, anyhow. See yuh later."

Before Lon or Jim could object to the plan, Cole was creeping off. He vanished, a vague, silent shadow. With the walls of the ranch house looming right before him, Cole's progress grew slower and slower. He realized perfectly that if his presence was discovered now, he would have but one chance in a hundred of evading the concerted gunfire that was sure to follow. Inch by inch he neared his objective.

Then, so suddenly that it brought him up with a jerk, the flat, thudding roll of a six-gun, wielded by a master hand, sounded through the night. Off to his left Cole could hear the speeding bullets chuckling and slamming into the corrals. Lon and Jim had not failed him.

The reply to the shooting came after a moment of strained surprise. From a dozen places answering lead whipped into the night, directed at the spot where that first six-gun had flamed. Cole did not worry about the two Texans being hit. Only a wild chance would bring that about.

That momentary pause between the finish of their shooting and the answer from the ranch, was enough to have allowed them to move several yards from their original position. And they were too old and tried a pair of frontier battlers not to know how to take care of themselves.

Cole was startled to see one rifle spitting flame from a window not ten yards away. Had he cared to, he was sure he could have cut down that particular defender. But to do so would have advertised his position, something he wanted to avoid above everything else.

Taking advantage of a slight lull in the shooting as the defenders reloaded, Cole covered the last few yards of his advance and, with a sigh of relief, stood upright, his back against the wall of the ranch house. So far, so good. For the moment, at least, he was safe.

For some time he stood in silence, listening alertly. He could hear the renegade in that nearby window, moving about and then he noted the metallic click of a loading gate as the shooter refilled the magazine of his rifle. A ghost of a smile twisted Cole's grim lips. What a startled individual that fellow would be, could he have known of Cole's proximity!

Cole stiffened. He heard voices, muffled and indistinct. He edged farther away from the window where the rifleman crouched. The farther he progressed in that direction the louder those voices became. Presently he realized that he was just beside another window and that in the room a heated conference was taking place. He recognized the heavy, grudging tones of Hack Orcutt.

"I tell yuh it's the biggest fool idee in the world—

holin' up here at my ranch, Partridge. What d'yuh expect to gain by it? Nothin' that I can see. We're surrounded an' we'll be wiped out like a lot of rats. Shore I'm sore. Who wouldn't be? I stand to lose everythin' now."

Then came Partridge's laugh, sardonic and mocking. "Quit your damn whining, Orcutt. It's too late now. Bridger knows you rustled some of his stock and blotted the brands. And then you were big enough fool to leave at least one of the critters in a place where he could hunt it out and examine that blotted brand."

"They'd never have found it if yuh'd gone a little slow in tryin' to grab possession of the range," retorted Orcutt. "But yuh had to start right in rushin' things. Naturally that got 'em up on their ears.

"They started lookin' around an' they stumbled on one of the critters before I had time to move them far enough away. Yuh cain't turn the world upside down in a couple of days, Partridge, an' yuh shoulda had sense enough to know it."

"That's neither here nor there," said Partridge crisply. "It was a gamble. I had to press matters. As soon as I heard of Raine forming that association I knew that the only possible chance for success was to move and move fast. I was in too deep to back down and so were you.

"Besides, we ain't beat yet. They'll have one devil of a job rooting us out of here and in case I have to I've got a joker to use on them. I've got the girl to use to bargain with them, you know."

A third voice broke in—the voice of Condon. "Jawin' back an' forth among ourselves ain't gonna help matters," rasped the bandit chief. "If yuh don't like the setup, Orcutt, what yuh gonna do about it? Any time yuh gamble for big stakes yuh gotta take a chance. We did—an' things kinda broke against us.

"But like Partridge says, we ain't discouraged or licked yet—not by a jugful. O' course we got one wild night ahaid of us. We'd be fools not to realize it. There's a lot of hard-boiled fightin' men out there. They're gonna start a squeezin' process, with us in the middle. But we're under cover an' they ain't. That puts the odds with us.

"An' if they'll feed up close enough that we can cut 'em down plenty, we'll be able to drive 'em off an' grab control of things. Then everythin' will be gravy. So get a hold of yoreself, Orcutt, an' quit whinin' an' snivelin' around. What if yore ranch does get shot up some? Ain't it worth it with the chance we got to make a pile?"

"Yeah—all that listens good, Condon," conceded Orcutt grudgingly. "But I'm tellin' yuh I don't like the feelin' of bein' cooped up thisaway. Yuh two are takin' too much for granted. Only one thing yuh said hits true with me, Condon, an' that is about the fightin' quality of those fellers outside.

"Partridge, I don't like this young jasper, Cole Bridger, any better than yuh do, but yuh got to admit he's a fightin' fool. Then there's those two Texans of Bill Raine's. They thought a lot of Bill, an' with him daid they're gonna be on the warpath proper. Me, I'd rather face a cage full of lions than I would Lon Sheer an' Jim Early when they're on the kill. Those guys ain't gonna be easy to lick—no, sir."

Partridge laughed. "I think those two Texans are a lot of bluff myself. They walk around looking hard and tough, but I don't know anybody in these parts who ever saw them pull a gun and use it. Yes, Bridger is a scrapper. But he's only one. I tell you if we cut down half a dozen of those fellows the rest will be more than willing to call it off."

"Don't agree with yuh, Partridge," said Condon abruptly. "Me, I think we got the edge in this, like yuh do. But I'm tellin' yuh that Lon Sheer an' Jim Early are tigers. Whip O'Conner ain't got a red haid for nothin'. Pat Ryan is tougher than rawhide an' Frenchy Gaston—like all slow-movin', slow-thinkin' jaspers—will be a terror when he once gets started. We got a scrap on our hands; don't fool yoreself about that."

In the thoughtful silence which fell after this remark, Cole moved closer to the window. A wild plan had come to him—an idea that took form in a slow, surging swell of anger at these cold-blooded schemers who were so very calmly talking over their chances to ravage the Punchbowl Hills range.

Cole had the three of them together now, all in the same room. Could he down them, the rest of the defenders would soon lose heart. It was a long gamble, but too good a chance to pass up. He drew his gun, savage satisfaction warming him at the solid feel of the smooth, cold butt. Stooping, he moved under the window, then straightened up slowly.

It was dark in there. The defenders were not fools enough to show any lights which might serve to outline them against the sights of the punchers outside. And Cole knew also that this absence of light would aid him just now. There would be no reflection to strike him and betray his position.

His head rose above the window-sill, his eyes searching the blackness within. His nostrils crinkled at the tang of tobacco smoke. Almost immediately he picked out the dim red pinpoint glow of a cigarette that somebody drew on, and brightened it. Good! He had one objective for his first shot. He would catch the others at the flare of the guns that he knew they would be quick to draw and use.

He leveled his gun; then he hesitated. If ever men needed killing, those three in the room did. But it was hard to shoot an unsuspecting man, regardless. Then Cole thought of Norma, of Bill Raine with his wounded head, of Sad Samson, of Tim Harding, Jack Batten and Spud Merrick. His jaw set and his lips thinned. This was no time for squeamishness. This was a battle for very existence. His gun steadied.

And just then, out of nowhere it seemed, a slinking shadow took sudden substance behind Cole; a heavy gun barrel lifted and fell. Cole crumpled in a heap, the whole universe blotted out by a livid blotch of color that danced before his eyes and vanished with the speed of a thunder-clap as consciousness faded.

XIII

THE SOUND OF THE BLOW, AND THE SLITHERING FALL OF
Cole Bridger's body, carried clear to the three men in
the room. In one move they were on their feet, backing
into separate corners, guns drawn and poised. For a
moment dead silence reigned. Then Flash Condon,
moving on his toes, slid along the wall toward the
opening. Just short of it he halted, peering intently as
he tried to pierce the outer blackness.

Presently a thin, triumphant voice spoke from the
window. "Keep yore shirts on, gents. This is Mogy
Evans. I got me a prize for yuh out here. I got Cole
Bridger—damn his eyes. Shall I plug him here or will
that attract too much notice?"

Partridge, Condon and Orcutt were dumb-founded.
At first they feared a trick of some kind. This sounded
like a fairy story to them. For how could it happen that
Cole Bridger should have approached so close to the
house without immediate detection?

"Hurry up," came Mogy Evans' impatient snarl. "He
may have some of his friends close around. I don't
want to get shot in the back. D'yuh want him inside or
shall I rock him off right here?"

Partridge recovered from his astonishment, his mind
moving swiftly, once he mastered his surprise. "Good
work, Mogy—fine work. Shove him through the
window to us. If we can keep on gathering 'em in this

way we'll have enough hostages to trade that other gang out of their eye-teeth. Grab hold, you fellows."

With Evans lifting and pushing and Flash Condon dragging, Cole's limp body was hauled into the room with Evans clambering swiftly in after. Partridge's first act was to kneel over Cole, scratch a match and make a quick survey. He pinched out the match and stood up.

"Mighty good work, Mogy," he said again. "How did you happen to nail him?"

"Things seemed sorta awful damn quiet an' threatenin' to me somehow," explained the viperish little gunman. "So I made the rounds of all the windows an' looked out good. I happened to catch sight of Bridger sneakin' along the wall. I didn't know it was him then, but I dropped out with my boots off an' sneaked after him.

"He stopped beneath that window an' listened to yuh dumb aigs jawin' together. He was so interested I got right up close. By an' by he pulls his gun an' begins to line down on one of yuh. So I up an' pistol-whips him. That's all. I'm beginnin' to wonder if I hadn't ought to have plugged him cold. What'cha gonna do with him?"

"Tie him up an' hold onto him," said Partridge. "I'm glad you didn't kill him just yet, Mogy. Dead, he wouldn't be worth a sou to us. As it is we can use him to trade, if the pinch gets too tight. But if he could sneak this close, others can do the same. Somebody who ought to be on watch is muffing the job. . . . Flash, you and Orcutt make all the rounds among the boys and tell 'em to wake up. . . . Mogy, get a rope and tie Bridger."

Thoroughly awakened to the fact that out in the soft, warm darkness vengeful men were creeping ever closer and closer, Condon and Orcutt departed on the run to warn the defenders. Evans brought to light a length of rawhide thong and bound Cole's limp wrists together, jerking viciously as he tightened the knots. With Cole's own neckerchief Mogy bound the equally limp ankles.

"Where'll yuh stow him, boss?" he asked.

"Right here is as good as any place, Mogy. I'm telling you again that you pulled a mighty slick trick; I won't forget you in the payoff. If the rest of this crowd were even half as brainy as you I'd lick the county till it yelled."

Partridge was clever enough to pander thus to the spiderish gunman's vanity, and Evans, though he affected nonchalance, swelled under the praise. "I'll go get my boots on an' then I'll come back an' watch this jasper," he announced. "He's one hombre I want to make shore of."

Lon Sheer and Jim Early waited a long time for Cole's return and as the time slipped into an hour, they became restless. "I got a hunch that lad's in trouble," murmured Lon, as they crouched in the dew-wet grass. "What say we move up an' try an' get a better line on things?"

"My own idee," agreed Jim. "Let's start."

The training of these two old-time rangers now

showed itself. Their advance was the acme of silence and speed. Vague and indistinct as wind-blown shadows, they slid forward. One moment it would appear that two long, flat bulks were upon the ground. Then they were gone, to appear ten yards farther on, only to disappear once more—intangible, unreal.

With the ranch buildings looming before them they worked around to the left, seeking the protection of the nearest corner of the angular stake and rider corrals. Somewhere close ahead someone coughed softly. Voices murmured. A third shadow slid down the fence and stopped beside the unwary renegades.

"Wake up, yuh hombres," came a rasping order in the voice of Flash Condon. "Those fellers are right up on top of us. Bridger reached clear to the house before he was discovered. Mogy Evans spotted him an' sneaked up on him. Mogy pistol-whipped him an' we got him tied up in the house. Partridge is gonna use him an' the girl as hostages to guarantee us a break if things get too hot. So watch yoreselves."

Lon Sheer nudged Jim Early with his elbow and rose to a crouch, his hands swung low along his thighs. "Yeah," he drawled coldly through the night. "Watch yoreselves. Hell's on yore heels an' yawnin' for yuh!"

Lon's announcement cut through the night like the icy whisper of death. It stupefied Condon and the group he had been talking to. Condon was the first to recover. Snarling a curse of warning, he snatched out his gun and dove for the shelter of the fence. But even while in midair two heavy slugs from Lon's big guns caught him and when Condon landed he was limp as a rag, his life torn from him.

A shrill, penetrating, Texas yell split the night. Five hundred yards away, up where he lay weakly upon the blanket spread for him, Bill Raine lifted himself upon one elbow, his old eyes shining and eager. Mig Almada was beside Raine and Mig's look was one of almost superstitious fear.

"Señor Raine," he burst out, "what een hell was that?"

"That means that Lon Sheer an' Jim Early are cuttin' loose at last, Mig. Heaven help the men who try an' face their guns tonight."

To the group of renegades in the corral, the flashing way in which Condon had been cut down and then that hair-raising yell, set their scalps to prickling. Startled into confusion, they hesitated momentarily. Before they could steady down, most of them were dead. For, sliding forward in crouching threat, Lon and Jim poured out lead in a thunderous roll.

These two wielded guns without apparent aim or even precision, yet they wasted not one shot. Their narrow-lidded eyes, trained by long years of stealthy night work along the Border, seemed to see with owl-like clearness. And they did not miss!

One man survived that deadly volley. He did so because he had sense enough to flatten out against the lower rail of the corral and stay there, motionless. The icy-eyed Texans reloaded their guns and moved forward slowly, alert to see that none of the group had any fight left in them.

Satisfied on this count, they resumed their stealthy way. They slipped low along the corral fence, keeping well down below the hail of return lead that came whipping from a dozen different points about the ranch where renegades were posted.

When they finally drew far enough away, the puncher who had feigned death to escape a real one, lurched to his feet and raced frantically for the ranch house. Calling a hoarse warning to the guardians of the place, he plunged inside.

"Where's Partridge an' Orcutt?" he gulped. "Where are they? Hell on wheels broke loose out there. Condon's daid an' half a dozen of the rest of the boys. Did yuh hear that yell? It's those two cold-eyed Texan devils—Sheer an' Early. Man, what wolves they are with guns! Where's Partridge, I'm askin' yuh?"

He was answered by Partridge himself, who came hurrying into the room with Orcutt behind him. "What's this?" he snapped. "Did I hear you say that Condon was dead?"

"Yuh did, Jay," gulped the terror-stricken puncher. "Daid as a mackerel. Them two Texans from the Half Diamond R are shore on the warpath. They surprised a bunch of us while Condon was givin' out some instructions, an' I'm tellin' yuh it was hell.

"It was like tryin' to face a couple of machine guns. They rocked Condon off the first rattle outa the box, an' they had the rest of the boys down before we knew what was happenin'. I ducked an' stayed down. I'd been daid, too, if I hadn't."

There was no ignoring the utter terror that showed in the puncher's stumbling words and staring eyes. Partridge's eyelids flickered and he ran the tip of his tongue across his lips. Orcutt had taken the news with a slow paling of features that went flaccid and slack with fear.

"Oh, my—" he began hoarsely, but Partridge cut him short.

"Shut up, Orcutt. Steady—all you men. Blinky, quit your sniveling like a scared kid. Those two hombres are only flesh and blood like the rest of us. A bullet well placed will stop them in their tracks. Get on the job, everybody, and try and land that bullet."

Partridge's brusk words struck through the momentary fear that had gripped the men in the room. They steadied and resumed their posts, vowing vengeance to the men who had killed Condon. Blinky, the lone survivor of the Texans' sudden and deadly sortie, shook himself like one trying to get free of dire thoughts.

"Where did they head, Blinky?" demanded Partridge.

"It was plumb dark an' I wasn't shore," stuttered Blinky. "But I think they went down around the corrals. I don't reckon they'll surprise any of the rest of the gang. After that shootin' the boys are on their toes."

"Of course," agreed Partridge with a confidence he did not feel. "They're liable to run against some lead any time."

167

Mogy Evans now came into the room. "Bridger's come to, boss," he twanged. "Yuh want to talk to him?"

Partridge nodded and followed Evans, taking Orcutt with him. Once out of earshot of those in the room, Partridge turned on Orcutt savagely. "You big yellow whelp," he snarled. "Don't you see that with Condon gone we got to keep the upper hand on his men?

"We'll never do it if we turn saffron and start to whine like you did. I'm getting good and tired of your spinelessness. If you don't cut it I'll wipe you out myself. That's a promise. Now stay with the men and fight."

Just as Partridge entered the room where Cole had been left, tied hand and foot, there came another menacing roll of gunfire, followed by that thin piercing Texas yell. In spite of his bravado, Partridge paled and knew an icy shiver of trepidation up his spine. He cursed harshly, as much to bolster up his own flagging nerve as anything else.

"So the mealy-mouthed polecat is ready to talk, eh?" he bit out viciously. "I'm telling you straight, Bridger, talking isn't going to do you much good. But spit it out. You haven't got much time."

Cole's voice came calmly from the blackness, where he was propped up in one corner. "I'll offer yuh a deal, Partridge. It don't concern me; it's about Miss Raine. Yuh turn her loose an' I'll sign over my ranch to yuh, plumb free and complete. How about it?"

Partridge laughed scornfully. "Not interested. Before

168

this deal is finished I'll have your ranch and your girl, too. I'll own this country, hombre. As far as signing anything over to me—that day is passed for you. Inside of the next few hours your signature won't carry an ounce of weight."

Again came that vibrant, Texan yell, broken by the rattling snarl of gunfire. Before the echo of it died out, a blast of shots ripped through the night from every side, bullets thudding and crashing into the house in a steady stream.

Partridge cursed in startled fury. The avenging circle was tightening, tightening. Cole Bridger laughed, and there was no mirth in the sound. "That don't sound to me like yuh were goin' to own anythin', Partridge—not a thing outside a six-foot hole in the ground.

"If yuh want to keep on whistlin' in the dark to keep yore courage up, fly to it. I'm tellin' yuh that yuh'll be wise to listen to my proposition."

Partridge hesitated. The death yell of one of his men echoed. He cursed again. "I still hold cards, Bridger," he snarled thickly. "If I do go you won't be here to see it. You'll be gone long before."

"Mebbe so," was Cole's quiet answer. "But just wait, feller, until Bill Raine gets his hands on yuh."

"Bill Raine!" exclaimed Partridge. "Why, Raine is dead!"

"Oh, yeah?" drawled Cole. "Guess again. He's far from it. He's outside runnin' this here clean-up of polecats. Evans didn't shoot as near center as he thought. He creased old Bill, that's all. Bill's plumb ripe an' fit

169

to haul on the rope that'll hang yuh, Partridge."

Mogy Evans slipped over beside Cole, a snarl on his lips. "Yuh're lyin', feller—yuh're lyin'. Just tryin' to get our goats."

"Think so if yuh want, Evans. Yuh'll be surprised."

This news had a peculiar effect on Partridge. Somehow he had figured all along that Bill Raine was the greatest obstacle between him and his mania for control of the Punchbowl Hills range.

He knew that Raine was a very powerful influence among the ranchers and a man of keen reasoning and dauntless courage. Partridge wanted to believe that his prisoner was lying, yet something in the cool, matter-of-fact way Cole spoke held a convincing ring.

A bullet from outside whipped through the window and chugged into an inner wall, narrowly missing Partridge. Cold sweat beaded the face of the schemer. There was something implacable, inescapable, about the way that invisible circle was tightening up about the ranch. He whirled on Evans in a flurry of rage.

"We'll find out whether Raine is alive or not. Send a man out to sneak through and have a talk with Raine, if he's alive. Tell him to spread the word that we've got Raine's daughter locked up here, and that if they want her turned back to them safe and sound they'll have to let us alone and treat with us. Otherwise, it will be the worse for her. Hurry up—get somebody started."

"I forgot to tell yuh, Partridge," broke in Cole steadily, "that all the boys out there agreed that there would be no prisoners taken. Yuh asked for this,

170

remember—murderin' Tim Harding and Jack Batten, an' burnin' the Half Diamond R Ranch.

"Yuh don't need to think any of yuh are gonna sneak clear now. The only man yuh can treat with is me—right here. If yuh want to talk business I might. . . . Remember, I said I might get some little break for yuh, such as a prison term instead of a rope or a gunful of lead."

Partridge panted in the dark like a crouching animal. He saw now, in a swift rush of clarity of thought, that he had made many mistakes in his vicious grab for power. The gravest one was in coming to the H Bar O Connected Ranch to make his stand against the forces of law and order.

It had seemed, with the combined forces of himself, Flash Condon and Hack Orcutt with their accumulation of men, that nothing the other ranchers could do would be sufficient to crush them. And with Norma Raine in his power besides, he felt he held all the winning cards in the deck.

Yet, over a period of a few short hours, much of the advantage had been drained away. Condon was dead, with several of his men. The circle was tightening, ever tightening. Orcutt had turned craven and the men were beginning to break. He still had the girl and he still had Bridger; but outside was grim, old Bill Raine—savage as a wounded grizzly, with men who had agreed to take no prisoners.

The contingent of men he had sent out to burn and loot had evidently been met and wiped out before their objective had gotten beyond the burning of the Half Diamond R outfit. Otherwise, the accumulation of fighting men outside would not have been so complete. For a certainty the tides of fortune had turned.

And now Partridge began to show his true colors— an egotistic, selfish individual. He had plotted from the first for his own gain and aggrandizement, using other men and their lives merely as tools to seek his own ends. It was characteristic that he should now turn all his thoughts to his own escape. He planned swiftly.

Vicious fires began to burn in him, fires of cruelty and revenge. By proper scheming there was a chance that he might break through the circle outside and win to freedom. But he would not go alone. Norma Raine would have to go with him.

And thus, in his feud with Bill Raine, his should be the final triumph. For no matter what victory Raine might gain, it would be empty and mocking if his daughter was not given back to his hungry old arms.

The attack had settled down to a steady, wicked pounding of gunfire. The night was one long rattle of report and echo. The impact of lead against the walls of the ranch house continued without a let-up.

Partridge could sense in the nervous and sporadic outbursts of shooting in reply, that the defenders were badly shaken of nerve and confidence. And at intervals came that long, shrill and mocking Texan yell, ever closer, ever triumphant.

Orcutt came rushing into the room. "Partridge," he

yelled, "yuh got to do somethin'. We cain't stand this much longer. There's three daid men in the south end of the house now. The place is gettin' all shot to pieces.

"Those damned Texans have cleaned up everybody in the corrals an' among the outbuildings. Yuh gotta do somethin', I tell yuh. We're gonna be cut down like rats in a trap. The men are ready to break an' I don't blame 'em."

Partridge made an unintelligible sound, not unlike the feral whimper of a blood-mad animal. He turned, whipped the automatic from beneath his armpit and drove two shots into the cowering Orcutt.

"You squealer, you sidewinder!" he rasped. "You yellow dog! I told you I'd finish you if you didn't quit whining."

Orcutt, his hands folded over his gross body, staggered almost across the room before he went down. Dying as he was, he had made an attempt to draw and return Partridge's treacherous lead.

But the paralysis of death struck him completely just as the six-gun cleared the holster. His forward movement as he crumpled, sent the weapon skittering across the floor through the inky blackness. It struck against Cole Bridger's outstretched feet.

"The jig's up, Mogy," rasped Partridge. "No use you an' me sticking around any longer. Only thing for us to do is try and make a sneak through. With luck and common judgment we might make it. We've got to try. I'm going to take the girl away with us right now.

"Bridger, here is your man. You caught him and

you've got a bigger grudge to settle with him than I have. Finish him off while I go get the girl. I'll tie her up and stuff a gag in her mouth. Soon as you're through here, come on along. She's in the room at the end of the hall. Make it fast."

"Okeh, boss," answered the gunman. "Be with yuh in a jiffy. Yuh got things figgered right. Yuh an' me for the open. Let those other fools take their medicine."

Partridge closed the door behind him, leaving Cole Bridger alone with a viperish killer who had vowed he would take the life of the man who had shot his brother.

XIV

To Norma Raine the night had been a strange medley of emotion. Since her supper had been brought her, no one had come near. With the deepening of darkness ideas of escape had come to her and she had tried fruitlessly several times to force the lock on the heavy shutters over the window.

Despairing of any chance at escape without help, she had paced the room tirelessly, striving to keep her thoughts practical and alive. The big battle was to fight off the sickening grief over her father.

When the first attacking volley crashed out through the night, Norma came up standing, her heart pounding with joy, her body tense with hope. And as the night moved on and the attack drew ever closer and more

174

sustained, fierce pride and satisfaction surged through her. But presently bullets began to bite through the walls of her room, and, wisely, she crouched almost flat on the floor, in a corner near the door.

Even when the hail of lead thickened until several times she was struck by flying splinters, she smiled. Chance alone would make one of those hurtling, leaden wasps strike her, and she was more than ready to chance such a thing, as long as ultimate victory was assured for the attackers.

Several times she heard men cry out, heard curses and sounds of muffled argument. Then, heavy and close, came two vicious, spiteful reports, followed by the thud of a falling body. Though she did not know it then, those shots were the two that had come from Partridge's automatic and the falling body had been Hack Orcutt, the traitor despised by those he had sided with, as well as those he had betrayed.

Norma heard footsteps soon after, footsteps that halted outside her door. She got to her feet, and drew up defensively. The lock clicked and the door squeaked open. She heard someone panting excitedly.

A match scratched and flared for a fractional moment, long enough for her to make out the snarling, savage features of Jay Partridge. The moment he located her, Partridge leaped. Norma tried to dodge, but one of his outstretched hands settled upon her shoulder, cruel as a vise.

"You're coming with me," he snapped. "Don't fight or it'll be the worse for you."

Norma, however, did fight, with every ounce of lusty strength she possessed. She kicked and scratched and flailed away like a fury. Her free hand found a grip on Partridge's neck and she dug her finger nails in his skin tenaciously. With a curse of pain he jerked free and his fist lashed out. It was a cruel, vicious blow which struck Norma on the side of the head. She crumpled, limp as a kitten.

With a grunt of relief, Partridge gagged her, slung her across his shoulder, and prowled cautiously out of the room. It would not do for him to let any of the defenders, aside from Mogy Evans, see him in this break for freedom.

If he was discovered, he could expect to be shot down like the human rat he was proving to be. After being led into this death trap, none of the renegades would take kindly to seeing the man responsible for their predicament, making a getaway while leaving them to hold the bag.

A muffled, heavy report sounded in the room where Mogy Evans was with Cole Bridger. Partridge found time to peel his lips back in a wolfish grin. That shot marked the end of another man he hated. Partridge waited a moment outside the door of that room.

"Mogy," he called softly. "Hurry up, man. We've got to make this fast."

The door swung open slowly and a man stepped out. At the same moment the door at the far end of the hall swung back and through it lunged one of the renegades, cursing.

"Partridge! Evans!" he yelled out. "Damn yuh, get up here an' help us fight. That gang's ready to break in. We cain't hold 'em off much longer. Yuh're in this as much as any of us—more for that matter. Get in here an' fight."

Partridge knew that he and Evans could not stand the risk of being discovered in their act of desertion, by any of their own crowd. To do so would mean having their fellows turn on them like savage wolves. So, he did not hesitate. His gun was in his hand at the moment the fellow broke into the hall. Deliberately he lifted it and shot, cursing as the lead went slightly off line from a center shot, due to the swaying weight of the limp figure across his shoulder.

The flare of the gun lit the hall up briefly and Partridge saw his victim go down, writhing from a smashed shoulder. He did not pause to shoot again. Too much shooting inside might draw others of the outlaw crowd. He whirled and lunged down the hall and through another door, and across the room beyond. But one frantic thought alone possessed him now—that of escape.

He stumbled to the window of the room and found it open. He lowered the senseless girl to the ground outside and crawled out himself. He listened a moment before hoisting her to his shoulder again and starting off.

A certain animal-like cunning came to him. He moved through the night softly, crouched low. He saw guns winking and flaming all about him. Heading for the spot where the line seemed thinnest, he kept up his steady pace.

An idea came to him which gave him renewed hope, and his pace increased. He became aware of the figure of a man not far to the right of him, a man who was levering measured shots from a Winchester rifle.

"Where's the nearest water?" he growled, his voice muffled and indistinct. "One of the boys is wounded bad. I'm luggin' him to water."

The man with the rifle spat deliberately. "Back yonder where Bill Raine is waitin', there'll be some of it," was the reply.

Partridge resumed his way unaccosted. He had no idea where Bill Raine was, but wherever that might be, it was the one place he wanted to keep away from. He hurried his pace to a stumbling run. Time was precious.

Before him several dark bulks snorted and milled uncertainly. Horses! Evidently they had been left there by the punchers as they began closing in. Partridge drew his automatic again, to dispose of anyone who might have been detailed to guard the animals. But evidently the lure of the battle had been too strong, for such a guardian had not been left. The horses were alone, fully saddled and ground-reined.

Savage exultation swayed Partridge, as he selected two of the faster looking animals. He tied Norma, who was beginning to regain consciousness and struggle a little, across one saddle, then swung up himself and whirled away through the night, leading the other horse behind. He headed east, toward the vague, black line that marked the distant palisades of Table Mountain.

When Partridge had placed a mile or two behind him with no immediate sound of pursuit, he began to breathe easier—to take stock. Some of his old confidence came back to him. The tempo of his reasoning picked up. He saw quite readily that the big plan of mastery of the Rhyolite County range was done for. His organization was shattered, his forces broken. Of the original plotters, only himself and Mogy Evans were left. Mogy would be satisfied. He had given Mogy his reward. He had left him with the man he hated, Cole Bridger—to finish off as he saw fit.

Partridge's lips peeled back in a harsh grin. The cattlemen had won—yet they had lost, also. Partridge knew now that Mogy Evans had missed, by half the width of a hand, in his attempt to kill Bill Raine. But the little gunman would not fail that way as far as Cole Bridger was concerned. And he himself, had the girl—Bill Raine's girl. And in those two things, Partridge could appreciate how the cattlemen had lost. Bridger and the girl. And all the range and cattle they might have saved could not make up for the loss of these two.

Behind him he heard the girl moaning, jerky, gasping moans, as the hard saddle seat, above the rack and pound of her horse's shoulders, beat against her limp, dangling body.

It was not pity for her misery that caused Partridge to rein in, dismount and go back to her, for there was no pity in his make-up for anyone now. But he knew, if he was to win clear, that speed and sustained travel alone were the two things necessary. And to stand that speed and sustained travel, the girl would have to be permitted to sit upright in her saddle.

With swift, tearing jerks, he loosed the ropes that tied her across the saddle. She struggled weakly, sliding to the ground. Partridge gave her a moment of rest, while he strained his ears for some sound of pursuit. The night, after the clamor that had engulfed the H Bar O Connected ranchhouse, seemed very still.

He reached over and jerked the girl to her feet. He shook her, slapped her lightly, first on one cheek, then on the other.

"Snap out of it," he grated harshly.

When she stiffened and beat weakly back at him with clenched fists, he knew that she was all right. He threw her into the saddle again, jerked her ankles down and tied them to the cinch rings. Her wrists he tied to the saddle horn. Then he was astride once more, lifting the horses to a run.

He held to his original course, boring straight for the black, cold face of Table Mountain. He had a fairly good idea of the Table Mountain country. This inner edge had been used for sheep at one time. But further back was a wilderness, rough and broken, untouched by man—a country where there were no trails of any sort, aside from those cut by the mule deer, the coyote, the panther and the savage, lone traveling lobo wolf.

Once in those roughs, Partridge told himself, he

would take a lot of finding. Food was the one thing he would have to get and already a thought had come to him as how to beat this emergency. What had become of that pack of supplies Pancho had taken in, when he went to guard the girl? And what had become of Pancho? Partridge had no idea how the girl had managed to get away from Pancho, but he did know that Pancho had taken in a good supply of food. Mogy Evans had told him that. It was Partridge's gamble that the food would still be at the deserted sheep-herder shack.

The black face of the mountain rose higher and higher as the panting horses swept close to the stygian shadow of it. The slope of the ground turned upward, the pace of the horses slowed. Partridge turned to his right, paralleling the low slope. Shortly the animals dipped clattering into a narrow ravine or wash. Up this Partridge reined.

The horses scrambled and lurched, snorting when they stumbled over some boulder in the darkness. The rim of the mountain above was ragged here, forming an uneven pattern against the stars, which, by comparison with the black bulk of rock and sandstone seemed to grow larger and brighter.

Increasing altitude brought a chill into the air, but the horses dripped with sweat and the cadence of their panting sounded loud and gusty. Above, somewhere along the rim a coyote started to sing, but choked into abrupt silence as its keen ears and nostrils told of the approach of those clambering horses.

Slowly the rim seemed to lower. Then they were through the final notch and the great flat mass of the mountain top lay spread cold and starlit before them. Here a wind was blowing, a sharp, icy wind, full of the pungent balsam of piñon and juniper and digger pine.

Partridge called another halt, reining back beside the girl. He found her sitting stiffly in her saddle, her head prideful—high, her expression stony.

"Well," he taunted—"it seems I win, after all."

Norma Raine shrugged. "There is tomorrow and a thousand more tomorrows. Men will ride steadily through all of them—if necessary. Sometime, some-where, they will come up with you. Then we'll see who wins."

Partridge laughed. "But how about you?"

"I don't really matter—as you'll find out in the long run. Your particular breed know only one real horror— and that is the hand of death. Tonight that nightmare struck you once, and you turned craven and cowardly. You left the men you had misled to die—while you ran. The chill of death was on you then, and you know it. Nothing you were able to do could keep such men as Cole Bridger, Lon Sheer, Jim Early and others from driving in, driving in—their guns reaching closer and closer to you all the time. You can't stop them now. You'll never stop them until they get you. You'll have time to think about it—now. The time will come when you'll be half crazy for sleep, yet fear that very sleep itself—fear it because when you wake from it, you may find the guns of retribution looking you in the eye.

No, Mister Jay Partridge—you've won nothing. You've lost."

Despite himself, Partridge was shaken. The girl had spoken almost in a monotone, like one in a trance of soothsaying. He cursed. "Don't talk of Cole Bridger following me. Bridger is dead by this time, damn him! I left him with Mogy Evans to finish—and that is a job that Mogy has been looking forward to. He won't bungle it."

This vicious information was like a knife thrust to Norma. She gasped. And Partridge laughed again.

"Didn't know that, did you? Well, we had Bridger in the ranchhouse back there. He thought he was good. He was going to crawl right into the place. But Mogy outfoxed him. He caught Bridger just about to crawl in a window and he pistol-whipped him. We had Bridger all tied up nice and tight in a room not far from yours. And when I pulled out with you, Mogy was just going in to blow his head off. Mogy might have bungled the job on your old fool of a father—but he won't miss Bridger."

Norma cried out, in mingled fear and relief. "My father! Then—Evans didn't—kill him!"

Partridge twisted angrily. He had not meant to let her know that. But it had slipped out. "If the knowledge will do you any good—no, he didn't kill him," he snapped. "He just creased him. But that won't go for Bridger. Bridger is through, and you better believe it."

Norma laughed, a little hysterically. She was emotionally drunk, her nerves jangling and screaming under the impact of this seesawing of information and misinformation. She had believed her father dead— had held his bloody head in her very arms. And yet this fiend beside her was saying that he was not dead. With the same breath he told her that Bridger, Cole Bridger was done for. Perhaps that also was a lie.

"But you did not see Cole Bridger die," she cried. "And at first you thought my father was dead. Now you say that he lives. And if he did not die, then Cole Bridger will not die. But you shall, Jay Partridge—you shall! Oh, there is Divine justice in all this madness. At every turn you are beaten. In the end you shall be beaten."

Now she began to sob, and it was well for her that she did. For it brought relief to those emotions which were punishing her so.

Little did she realize the effect of her words on Partridge. They brought the demon of doubt leering at him. True, he had heard a single gunshot in the room where Bridger lay securely bound and it had seemed reasonable to believe that Mogy Evans had fired that shot. But now he also remembered that he had taken time to call one more warning to Evans—to tell him to hurry up. But—Mogy Evans had not answered—or appeared!

For the first time the significance of this struck fully home. Back at the ranch he had been too engrossed in his own efforts at escape to grasp or consider that significance. But the full force of it hit him, now.

Perhaps this girl was right—perhaps Mogy had bungled that last job. Perhaps Bridger was not dead, after all.

And he had lost, all along—lost in the vital things. A slip here—a slip there. Nothing had worked as he had planned. He cursed again, like a madman—cursed the earth, the sky, the distant paling stars, which seemed to mock him in their slow, inscrutable wheel across the heavens.

Cruelly he rowelled his bronco into surging movement, yanking Norma's mount into a run behind him.

Across the flat breast of the mountain the horses pounded, hurdling rocks, crashing through brush. And in the east the sky was turning a clear, warm gray, with just a hint of rosy light to announce the approach of dawn.

Daylight was at hand as they clattered down into the little basin, where stood the sheep-herder shack. Two slinking gray shadows, which had been standing over a dark, sprawled blot not far from the cabin, slid up the slope and were gone. Norma glimpsed them—and saw the dark figure over which they had stood. She shuddered. A dead man! Pancho, the Mexican. Coyote bait.

Partridge had seen the same thing and he reined his snorting horse over beside the sprawled figure. Norma shut her eyes tightly.

Partridge did not note the girl's reaction. In the dead Mexican he saw only one more example of the way his plan had miscarried, another ominous reminder of failure. If he had puzzled any over the how and why of Norma's escape from the Mexican in the first place, he gave no evidence of it now.

Partridge looked past the dead Mexican and over at the pile of equipment, which lay just as Pancho and Mogy Evans had unloaded it in the first place. And, best of all, on the smear of scant green grass below the spring, stood the very pack horse that had carried in the supplies.

Partridge shook off the mood of failure. Here was food, blankets, and the means of transporting them, right at hand. Almost directly ahead, on into the east, was the untrod wilderness of Table Mountain, where sanctuary and escape might be waiting. Enough of these doubts and fears engendered by the ravings of a hysterical girl. What matter it that one of his men lay dead almost at his very feet? What matter it that his infamous organization was shattered and broken, his great idea nothing more than a bloody phantasy? He had food and transportation, and the whole wide world to hide in. And he had the girl.

A fury of industry gripped the renegade gambler. He rode over to the supplies and dismounted there. He caught the pack horse, brought it up and cinched the saw-buck pack-saddle into place. He stowed the pack, threw a diamond hitch, then climbed into his own saddle once more.

He was weary and the saddle mounts gaunt and flank nipped with fatigue. But this was neither the time nor place to stop and rest. Somewhere back in those distant, wild roughs, but not here. He spurred his mount into movement.

Five minutes later all was still and motionless in the little basin—as still as the dead man who guarded it. And the bland sun rose to wonder at it all.

XV

WHEN COLE BRIDGER LISTENED TO THE RUTHLESS, cold-blooded agreement between Partridge and Mogy Evans, as Partridge delegated Evans to murder Cole with no more compunction than if he were a mad dog, he knew that the greatest crisis of his life lay before him. Evans would glory in this chore.

In the warped, twisted soul of the treacherous little gunman there existed not one iota of honor or mercy. He hated Cole venomously; hated him because Cole had shot down his brother. Evans did not consider that his brother Claude had been killed by a better man, a faster man, while Claude was playing the skulking coward and dry-gulcher.

He only knew that by Cole's hand had his brother died, and the desire for vengeance was eating at the soul of him like corrosive acid. Cole knew that Evans would shoot him as he lay there, trussed hand and foot, without giving him the slightest semblance of an even break.

On top of this, Partridge was planning to carry

Norma Raine away with him, to a future that Cole did not even dare think of, lest he become entirely mad with futile rage and desperation. This was a time for thought, the fastest thought he had ever stirred his wits to.

There was one slight hope, and that lay in Hack Orcutt's gun, which had skidded, unnoticed through the darkness, against Cole's outstretched feet. Yet, Cole's hands and feet were bound.

As Partridge left the room Cole made his plan—long, dangerous gamble though it was. Yet it was all that was left to him. He twisted his feet tightly back and by a prodigious effort, lifted himself to his knees, the bottoms of his feet thus braced against the wall behind. He sensed the position of Evans and he estimated swiftly the distance which lay between them.

He heard Evans step closer to him, heard the click of a gun lock as Evans cocked his weapon. "Well, feller," snarled the gunman, his voice thick and husky with savage, animal-like fury, "I reckon yuh know what I'm gonna do to yuh—an' why. Yuh're about to grab a harp. Inside of ten seconds yuh'll be a daid man. Happy thoughts to yuh!"

Cole knew that the deadly muzzle was steadying, aligned with his heart. Seconds marked the gap between life and death. With a silent, grim prayer to the gods of luck and righteousness, Cole snapped his knees straight. He drove himself forward low and hard, using the wall as a base of leverage behind his thrusting feet. From the top of his head to his toes,

Cole's entire body was as tense and set as a log of wood, a human catapult.

As he lashed out through the blackness, he felt the bottom of the butt of Evans' outstretched gun slide off the back of his head, heard Evans' involuntary curse of surprise. Then his head smashed into the pit of the gunman's stomach with every ounce of his muscular body behind it.

As Cole rolled on the floor after the impact, half-dazed and with his neck aching from the terrific force of the blow, he heard a strange conglomeration of gasps, choked groans and blubbering curses. He heard the tattoo of Evans' heels beating on the floor as the gunman writhed and tumbled in the terrible agony of strange convulsion that grips a man who has been delivered a knockout blow in the solar plexus.

Cole wasted little time in wondering. So far his desperate plan had worked successfully. But he was still bound and seemingly helpless and Evans might recover at any time.

Over and over rolled the young rancher toward the place he had been a moment before. His hip struck a hard, angular object that gouged him painfully. He squirmed until his hands found Orcutt's gun, and with the hard, cold grip of it firmly clenched, a sense of ultimate victory grew upon him.

He did not hesitate a moment in performing the next act of this desperate break for life, freedom and the culmination of love. Thought of Norma spurred him to the cold ruthlessness that alone could save them both. He rolled over and over again, until he collided with the still gasping and tumbling gunman. Twisting slightly, and shooting entirely by feel and blind calculation, Cole pushed the gun muzzle against Evans' side and thumbed the hammer.

At the heavy, muffled report, Evans' gasps cut off abruptly; his body shivered slightly and lay still. The most repellent part of Cole's task still lay before him, but he did not quail. Anything was justified. He rolled himself across Evans' legs, twisted until his back lay over the gunman's waist and his hands might fumble about the other's belt.

Cole was gambling deeply. A killer of Evans' caliber would probably pack a concealed Bowie knife upon his person somewhere, depending on its aid to meet some desperate emergency which might crop up. Cole's gamble still held good. He located the haft of the knife under the gunman's shirt and after a moment of work, got it free.

He felt slightly sick as he rolled to the floor once again. Harsh and terrible as was his mood, the true spirit of honor and humanity was strong in him. He hoped he would never have to rob a corpse again.

Cole rose to a sitting position and bore his full weight upon the haft of the Bowie knife, forcing its point deep into the soft pine floor. When it stood firmly he pushed the buckskin thong which held his wrists hard against it, sawing up and down.

The knife was keen, and a moment later Cole's hands were free. Another slash of the knife and his ankles were likewise rid of their bonds. Locating Orcutt's gun again the young rancher rose to his feet, shook himself, drew a deep breath and stepped out into the hall.

Just a moment before there had been a heavy, smashing report in that hall. And there had been someone yelling and cursing at Evans and Partridge. Now there was only a pocket of blackness, pungent and eye-smarting with powder smoke. That, and someone groaning on the floor.

Cole stood motionless. What had happened in this hall? Who had shot who? Was it Partridge down there on the floor, groaning? Had one of his own men turned on the renegade and cut him down?

Cole gambled. He had to know. For Partridge was his man. Free once more, a ready gun in his hand, Cole knew now that the trail lay straight and true before him. It was a trail which could have but one ending. No matter where that trail led, nor how long or many the miles of it might be, it could lead to only one ending. Partridge! And, at that ending either he or the renegade gambler would go down, finally and for all time.

He would free Norma of course, before he left. He would get her out of this charnel house and safely back in the arms of her father. After that—Partridge!

But perhaps this was Partridge on the floor beside him. With his left hand Cole fumbled and found a match. He stepped away from the wall and with his left arm fully outstretched, dragged the match across the wall until it sputtered into light, and he held that light at arm's length, in case this wounded man would shoot at it.

But no shot came and the match flared brighter, bringing into relief the pain-twisted features of the man on the floor. It was not Partridge, but those lips began muttering Partridge's name, cursing it.

"You rat—you crooked, double-crossin' rat. Yuh're yellow, Partridge. Yuh're aimin' to make a run for it— with that damned girl. An' yuh're leavin' the rest of us here to die—the men who fought for yuh an' stuck by yuh through it all. Go ahaid—plug me again. I don't give a damn—yuh know what I think of yuh."

Cole dropped on his knees beside the wounded outlaw, the match going out. He caught the fellow by his sound shoulder, shook him.

"This ain't Partridge," he snapped. "This is Bridger—get that—Bridger. I'm after Partridge—an' when I get him I'll square yore debt as well as my own. What did yuh say about him runnin' off— desertin' the rest of yuh—an' takin' the girl with him? Is that right?"

A talon hand fumbled and found Cole's wrist, gripping it tightly. The wounded man spoke thickly, but more coherently than he had at first.

"Lemme get this right. Yuh say yuh're Bridger— Cole Bridger? But it was Partridge who shot me—the skunk. I saw him plain, when his gun flared. An' he had that Raine girl over his shoulder. He was packin' her off. He was haidin' for that door at the other end of the hall when I busted in on him. He shot at me across

192

his body—movin' when he shot—an' that's all that kept him from gettin' me center."

Cole's voice was bright and chill. "Yuh're shore of that? This ain't delirium—yuh're clear haided enough to know what yuh're sayin' an' who yuh're sayin' it to?"

"Dead certain. Yuh're Bridger. Yuh're after Partridge, the double-crossin' snake who shot me. Partridge had the girl. I'm givin' it to yuh straight, Bridger—so help me. Partridge is makin' a run for it—an' he's got the girl. Go get him, Bridger. An' when you come up with him, tag the name of Luke Harmon on the first slug yuh throw into him. Go get—"

But Cole was already gone, following the draft of the open door at the end of the hall. By this same chill fanning of the searching night wind he found the open window. He clambered out, pausing for a moment as he listened and stabbed searching eyes into the darkness.

Cole thought fast in those next fleeting seconds. There was no doubt but that Partridge would try and break through the circle of vengeful ranchmen and punchers. Obviously, the first thing to do was to reach that circle and spread the alarm, so that the men would keep an extra careful watch for the slinking woman stealer.

Decided on this, Cole ran straight out away from the ranch buildings. Hardly fifty yards had he gone when a pencil of flame licked out through the night and a bullet snapped by his head.

"Hold it!" he yelled. "This is Bridger. I just made a getaway. Hold it!"

A startled, overjoyed curse of surprise greeted his warning. "Come a-runnin', Bridger," was the answer. "Glad to see yuh. When word got around that they had captured yuh, none of us ever expected to see yuh alive again. Didn't think Evans would pass up that chance to plug yuh."

"Didn't think so myself," panted Cole, as he came to a stop beside the puncher, "but I beat Evans to it. Close shave, but I made it. Orcutt an' Flash Condon are daid. I'm lookin' for Partridge. He's got Miss Raine with him, and he's tryin' to break through our lines. Pass the word along to be on the lookout for somebody packin' another person—"

The puncher broke in with curses of dismay. "I'm a fool!" he stormed. "A blind, dumb fool! Why, Bridger, a feller went by me not two minutes ago. I saw he was packin' somebody over his shoulder, but in the dark I couldn't make out that it was a girl. He talked kinda low an' husky, explainin' that he was packin' out one of our boys who had been wounded. He—"

"Which way did he haid?" snapped Cole, silently cursing the puncher for his mistake. Yet he wasted no time in openly upbraiding the honest and remorseful chap. "Which way?"

"Due east right over there." The puncher pointed. "I'll go with yuh. He cain't be far."

"You stay put," ordered Cole crisply. "This is my chore and I'll get him."

The puncher started to speak again, but Cole did not hear him. He was gone, loping through the darkness like a wolf on the trail. Some two hundred yards further on he stumbled into a group of horses. He selected a mount, surged into the saddle and raced away.

It was good to feel the smooth firmness of saddle leather again, to balance to the leap and plunge of horseflesh beneath him. The beat of the night wind, humming by his ears, swayed him with exultation. The tangled trail had at last straightened out.

There were no more cross-currents to consider; no more false leads, trickery or deceit to battle. All that was behind. Ahead lay the culmination of the entire mad convulsion which had blighted the Punchbowl Hills range.

The cause of it all was out there, somewhere in the night, fleeing like the craven coward he was. With him he had dared to carry away the strongest force that had ever entered Cole Bridger's life—Norma Raine, the girl he loved.

It was fitting, Cole concluded, that the final issue should lie between himself and Partridge. It was fitting that chance, or fate, or whatever it might be called, had selected him to ride Partridge to earth and mete out the punishment due. So be it.

A coyote, slinking hunter of the night, having sated its hunger on the carcass of a luckless rabbit, sought a rising point of ground to wail its age-old loneliness to the austere stars. Yet, even as it pointed its slim snout to the heavens and began the whimpering prelude to its song, it suddenly flattened to earth, ears pricked, eyes growing slant and green. Just a wraith of movement, it slid from sight behind a bush, where it listened and watched.

Through the night two horses came thundering, panting by in furious effort. On the leading one was the figure of a man—a man who bent low over the saddle-horn, alternately peering eagerly ahead and glancing fearfully back. On the horse he led was a slim figure, bound to the saddle, humped with misery.

They vanished into the blackness, leaving behind the tang of new-turned, dew-moistened dust, and the reek of sweating horseflesh. The coyote's sensitive nostrils twitched, and its lips lifted in a half-formed snarl, its eyes narrowing with instinctive fear and hatred.

Wariness bred through the centuries, held the coyote to its hiding place, long after the echo of those speeding horses had died. And then, because the night once more seemed to belong to it, the coyote again sought the open, its eerie cry taking form in its throat. Yet, once again that song did not get beyond the preliminary whimper. Again the coyote whirled and sought a covert.

For, out of the night another horse came rushing, carrying still another of the hated man creatures. This man did not look back. Straight ahead he peered, lean jaw set, eyes bleak and cold; then he was gone. Long the coyote slunk low, and Cole Bridger was entirely out of hearing when the animal finally found voice to the nameless urge within it.

Cole never hesitated in his guess as to the goal of the fleeing Partridge. It would be the far-flung, gaunt and rugged crest of Table Mountain. It seemed to Cole that he was following the trail more by instinct than anything else. An inner consciousness of some sort drew him onward, dictated when and where to turn. So powerful was this subconscious guidance, he never thought of questioning it.

Cole had never penetrated the interior wilderness that lay distant miles beyond the rim of Table Mountain, but he had heard men tell of its vastness, its harshness, its million coverts where a fugitive might hide. However, he was not daunted. He was confident of his superior condition, his superior knowledge of the open, his superior ability of trailing. Partridge could not elude him, not if he traveled to the far corners of the world.

Cole looked at the stars, at the horizon straight ahead. He was gratified to note that the stars had paled perceptibly, and that a dim translucence, a hint of silver, lay beyond the eastern rim of the world. Dawn was hovering.

The trail led through tangled brush, which cloaked the gradually rising flanks of the mountain, leading ever closer and closer to the stark, black cliffs. It turned slightly south for a time, then angled east once more. It grew darker, so it seemed, with the shadow of the cliffs lying cold. Abruptly Cole's mount dipped into a crooked, steep-walled arroyo. It began to climb.

It seemed as if he was traveling through a tunnel, which by some legerdemain of nature had suddenly had the top third of it lifted off completely. The bronco began to labor slightly, as the pitch of the arroyo grew sharp, piercing directly into the breast of the palisades. The walls reared higher and higher. The trail no longer lay in the bottom of the rift, but began angling up the side, narrow and treacherous.

Cole left things entirely to his bronco, knowing that the sure-footed animal could progress more safely if left to its own devices. A chill wind whipped through the cut, the living breath of vastness and illimitable distance—rich with the odor of pungent growing things.

The world grew lighter. Dawn was flaring now, whirling its banners of rose and silver across the sky. Abruptly the trail led clear of the precipitous cleft and Cole found himself atop the violet crest of Table Mountain.

A single glance he threw to the west. The world out there was still shrouded in the reluctant shadows of early morning, but cutting through them reared a distant pillar of lurid flame. At first the sight of this drew Cole taut and wondering. Then he understood and fierce exultation whipped through him.

That was the H Bar O Connected Ranch burning; the last stronghold of the destroyers being wiped out. This meant only one thing. Those indomitable, dauntless men down there—Bill Raine, Lon Sheer, Jim Early, Mig Almada—had shot their way to victory. They had done a job and done it well.

Only for Cole was the trail not yet ended. To him alone had been given the last and biggest job of all. He whirled his mount and thundered away, using the light of day to pick out Partridge's trail.

Sunrise showed Cole a harsh, scantily brushed world, bland and colorless and nearly flat near about, but piling up into timber shrouded roughs, far out there to the east. It was difficult to pick up the trail here. The subconscious certainty that had guided Cole through the first part of the chase had left him. Here the world was too vast and rough. From now on it was up to the cunning of searching eye and cold judgment. The ground showed large areas of nearly naked rock and on this a horse's hoof left little sign.

But Cole's concentration to the task was that of a trailing animal. He missed nothing. A slight gouge here, a scratch there, was enough to give him his direction, and he pushed steadily ahead.

In the morning light his face appeared haggard, lined, and set with a great weariness. Sleepless hours, end on end, had caused his eyes to sink far into their sockets, but had not in the least dimmed their intent, icy flicker. The sun beat on his uncovered head, but he paid no heed.

His horse was gaunt with weariness also. The spring had gone from its stride; its pace reduced to a shuffling jog. Cole did not urge the faithful beast to excess, for the chase was not a matter of sheer speed any longer. It had become a test of endurance now, with the quarry intent upon leaving a tangled trail and the pursuer intent on ferreting the same trail out.

Those horses ahead would be feeling the pace also, and to Partridge would fall the nerve-wracking tension of the fugitive, on whose trail followed a remorseless, inescapable fate. An element of gambling lay in the strategy of Cole's planning. How long would Partridge be able to stand the strain? How long before his ragged nerves and quailing spirit would snap and cause him to turn and fight instead of run?

For Cole knew that Partridge was not fool enough to believe there would be no pursuit. Nothing in the world could have promised such a relentless vengeance as the carrying off of Norma Raine. Partridge would know that if but one man was left alive in the loyal forces of the big conflict, that man would take his trail now—to follow it to a final finish. Yes, Partridge would know that, and always would his back trail be a silent unspoken threat to him.

Cole could guess what the terrible strain of being followed, relentlessly followed, would be like. He could guess how even the most craven coward in the world would finally break before the hovering threat, and would whirl and snarl and fight back. Sooner or later, Partridge would do this.

Cole drew and examined the gun that had once been the property of Hack Orcutt. It had served Cole well, so far. He spun the cylinder, flipped open the loading gate and ejected the empty shell that had taken the life of Mogy Evans. He thumbed a fresh, fat, yellow cartridge into the yawning cylinder.

Now the ground was not so rocky, and, though the brush began to thicken, the trail lay easier to follow, gouged into the earth which gave life to that brush. It led straight east, deeper and deeper into the fastnesses of the mountain.

Abruptly a small, nearly circular basin opened before him. Down there Cole saw a cabin, a warped, ramshackle affair, sprawled uncouthly at the edge of a group of junipers. Green grass showed in a smear near it, signifying the presence of water.

Carefully Cole studied the layout for some sign of life. But it lay, still and deserted, except for a group of buzzards, flapping clumsily about some object near the cabin. Cole rode down.

At his approach the buzzards drew reluctantly aside, perching on nearby junipers. One flapped a heavy way to the roof of the cabin. With naked, red, repellent heads out-thrust, they fixed beady eyes on this intruder.

A gust of warming wind whipped Cole's nostrils and he gasped, then held his breath. He reined his horse away from that horror on the ground where the buzzards had been feeding. The end of Pancho, the Mexican, had indeed become an ignominious one.

Cole dismounted beside the cabin and looked in, to see only littered emptiness. He went on to the spring, where he lay flat and drank thirstily. Then, while his mount slaked its thirst, he began circling on foot. He soon picked up the trail again and marked its direction with grim thoughtfulness. Partridge had taken to the roughs.

That drink of water, aside from killing Cole's thirst, had only emphasized the fact that he had not eaten for hours and hours. The pangs of hunger tore at him. Stoically he pulled up his belt another notch or two, then went back to his horse. In another minute he was once more on the trail, crowding ahead into the roughs.

XVI

THOSE WHO HAD EMPHASIZED THE FORBIDDING ruggedness of the Table Mountain roughs, had not exaggerated. Cole Bridger had seen his share of country, good and bad. But he had never faced anything the equal of which he now had, through the long hours of that fateful day, been battling.

Here it seemed that Nature had deliberately builded to repel all but Her own creatures of the wild. Here the world was one gigantic pattern of canyon and ridge—the one deep, cavernous, cold, where rushing streams battered a foaming way over cruel, gleaming, naked boulders—the other incredibly steep, where towering, gloomy conifers clung in stubborn ranks to all but the jagged, barren rocky spines of the crests.

Cole's horse toiled and lurched and gasped up one heart-breaking slope, only to find the trail leading across one of those rocky crests to plunge down another slope equally steep and heart-breaking. Then, at the bottom, there were those foaming, riotous streams to cross, on greasy, slippery boulders that seemed to leer and wait for some misstep on the part of horse or rider.

Near mid-afternoon that misstep came. Cole was on foot, leading his mount, across a vicious tangle of boulders, through icy water that foamed nearly to his waist. He was crossing here, because Partridge had crossed here. There on the far bank the dank, moist earth lay black and scarified where horses had passed less than an hour before.

Cole had reached that far bank and was tugging at the reins as his pony floundered over the treacherous footing. It seemed that the crossing had been made in safety. But a slippery rock turned beneath one of the animal's hoofs. It stumbled, half fell, and scrambled wildly to keep its feet. And in that moment of turmoil, sharp above even the buffeting roar of the water, sounded an ominous crack.

The horse sagged slightly and it seemed that an almost human groan broke from it. With one more wild lurch it made the haven of the bank, but—the off front leg, just below the knee, swung limp and broken.

The horse stood, head down, shivering. Cole took a single look and his lips tightened. Regret, pity— clouded his eyes. But he did not hesitate. There was but one thing to do. He slid his gun free and the heavy rumble of it sent a flood of echoes rolling. The horse collapsed and lay still.

"It was kindness to you, little hoss," muttered Cole

huskily. "Yuh did yore best—and yore bones will be one more monument to that crooked, hell-born rat of a Partridge."

He bent, ran a hand over the gaunt, still shoulder then turned away and began to climb, the bitterness about his set lips increasing.

It was killing work. Each step was upward, lift and drive—lift and drive. When he had the chance, Cole used his hands, dragging at the rough bark of the conifers, or at the branches of delicate, mysterious mountain shrubs which seemed to thrive in those perpetual shadows.

Now, for the first time, his own condition came to haunt him. For what seemed uncountable hours he had not rested. It was æons since he had tasted food. Even the tough, rawhide consistency of muscles such as his, could not stand this neglect forever. And the best part of the day was gone—night and darkness but a few hours away.

This knowledge drove Cole frantic. He called on latent nerve forces, forces which drove weary muscles to their relentless bidding. He climbed and climbed and climbed. He reached another rocky crest, where that fresh turned trail cut through a narrow gap. And then he went down again, into still another of those remorseless gulfs, down to dank, water sprayed depths. But here he found an encouraging omen. It was a saddled horse, standing beside the water, standing on trembling legs wide spread and braced. Its head hung low, its eyes half closed. Its flanks were torn and crusted with dried blood, where spur rowels had bitten in viciously, again and again. Ah yes—there was weariness and exhaustion up ahead.

A glance told Cole that in this horse, Partridge had left nothing of aid to him. The animal was completely done. It was doubtful that it would ever live to find its way out of this country of gloom and shadows. Yet Cole lingered long enough to free it of saddle and bridle, maneuvers the animal seemed hardly to notice.

Then Cole crossed the water and went on. A gleam of comfort came to him. Without doubt the trail was growing fresher with every step. In places the black edges of the earth were still crumbling in about the hoof prints. And there were boot tracks in evidence also. Partridge was afoot. And now Cole understood the significance of what Partridge was doing with that extra horse. It must be a pack horse and a pack horse suggested food and other supplies. Where Partridge had gotten these things, Cole did not know. But he realized still more thoroughly now, how necessary it was to force this matter to a showdown, without let-up.

Also, he knew that Partridge must be cognizant that pursuit was close. Else it was conceivable that the renegade would have camped before this, rather than abandon that exhausted horse, back by that last stream.

So Partridge was afoot! This knowledge brought a new fund of strength to Cole. He drove up that tortuous slope like a mad man, drove and drove until his lungs seemed raw and until the salt sweat clouded his eyes and half blinded them.

A shrill, insistent yammering finally impinged itself upon his consciousness. He halted, panting, gasping, scrubbing the sweat from his eyes. As the pounding tumult of his heart quieted somewhat, he identified that squawking, up ahead. It was the cry of the mountain jay, that sleek, crested, blue-black inhabitant of the shadowy conifers, and the jay was scolding something that had disturbed the primeval silence of its mountain home. And Cole understood. His quarry was just ahead!

Traveling alone, without the necessity of herding a weary pack animal before him, he had closed the gap. He had caught up!

Flat on his stomach Cole dropped, peering up through the serrated boles of the conifers, toward the gleam of the sky beyond the next crest. And presently he saw them. A man on foot, staggering wearily, dragging at the lead ropes of two horses. On one of the animals sat a slim, humped figure, swayed low over the saddle horn with weariness. On the other a tarpaulin covered pack. Even as Cole watched, they passed from sight beyond the crest of the ridge.

Cole went up that killing slope like a hunting wolf. Exhaustion, weariness, hunger—all were behind him now—forgotten. It had been the sight of Norma Raine that galvanized him so.

He reached the crest of the ridge and peered down. Now he saw that here the topography of the country had changed somewhat. Here lay a curving basin, a huge horseshoe gouged from the breast of the mountain. As it sloped far down to the right it ended in a great canyon, blue and shrouded by its own terrific depths. But to the left the slope of land could be traveled by clinging close to a curving line of low cliffs. Straight ahead, a good two miles distant, the rim of the basin led out over another shoulder, where only the sky seemed to stand.

Down below, Cole could see his quarry. Partridge was slogging along like an automaton, bent almost double, as he leaned his weight against the lead ropes of the horses. Cole's heart went out to that hunched figure on the first horse, so slim, so helpless, bared head gleaming auburn in the slanting rays of a westering sun that struck through here fully. He murmured her name once—"Norma!"

Cole gauged the distance to Partridge. Too far to chance a shot with a six-gun. And now that he was this close, he did not want to risk a slip-up. Rightly played, the game was in his hands now.

He calculated the angle Partridge was traveling. He saw that the fellow evidently intended circling under that line of low cliffs. Cole knew what his move was. By going straight up this backbone and going fast, he could reach the breast of the mountain and circle out ahead. He could choose his own spot in one of those various chimneys that broke through the cliffs—and he could wait there. And then, when Partridge came even with him, where the range was short and the shot sure—there would be the finish!

Cole swung back far enough to be fully hidden. Then he went along the ridge at a run, skirting rocks, dodging timber, hurdling fallen stuff. He reached the main breast of the mountain and began his circle, keeping to the matted cover above the cliffs. He traveled like a man in a frenzy now, his sunken eyes gleaming with a sort of blank, deathless fire.

Once he stopped, crept to the cliff rim and looked over. He saw that he was already somewhat ahead of Partridge. But he went back and increased his lead to a good three hundred yards. Then he hunted for a way down from the cliffs. He reached a chimney that looked right and started down it. It was a precipitous task, but he lowered himself swiftly, using heels, toes, clawing fingers—even elbows and knees.

He halted once for breath and looked down. He saw that the bottom of the chimney opened behind a bulwark of brush. Perfect! His eyes gleamed brighter. Behind that brush he would wait—for Partridge!

He started down once more. He was aching all over from the strain now. The last thirty feet was almost like lowering himself on a rope, hand below hand. His bleeding fingers gripped at tiny ledges, at ragged outcrops, jagged rock points. Twenty feet from the bottom a clawing hand reached for another hold. It seemed solid enough. But as his full weight swung on it, the treacherous bottlerock split away. He felt it give, grabbed frantically for another hand-hold which was not there. He fell, angling downward. A bootheel, kicking inward, caught on the rock slightly, but instead of aiding it threw him sideways, and in that position he dropped the rest of the way, a full score of feet, smashing down on his hips and the broad of his shoulders.

The impact was terrific. A terrible agony ran along his spine. Then his whole body seemed to numb and become dead. The thin area of sky above him dimmed and became almost black. A thunderous roaring was in his ears.

Only the drive of an iron will kept Cole Bridger's senses from leaving him at that moment—only iron will and an indomitable inner consciousness which told him that he must not falter now—that the culmination of those terrific miles of pursuit was just before him—that he must make the final play or everything was lost.

That inner voice pounded at him, whipped him with a lash of fire. He set his teeth, drove the cold mists from his brain. Veins and cords stood out on his face, rippled the length of his straining throat. He moved— he rolled over on his face!

Clammy sweat drenched his entire being. Agony gripped him anew, waves of livid fire that seemed to shrivel his very soul. But he moved again. Somehow he got to his feet, stood upright on legs and feet that were like clubs—but he stood upright.

The world whirled and danced before his eyes. The earth seemed to drag at him, pull at him with a power of some terrible magnet. Yet Cole Bridger knew that if he gave way to that pull now he would never rise again.

The click of a steel shod hoof on stone crackled through his consciousness. He looked to the right, peering painfully through the fringe of brush which encircled him. And he saw his quarry, close now, moving along a line that would bring humans and horses close to his covert. Partridge was as he had seen him, back on that far ridge. Leaning over, dragging at those lead ropes, a malignant fiend of a man, his face a twisted mask, sodden with fatigue and the fear of retribution.

Cole saw Norma. Her head was on her breast, her eyes closed. She rode like one asleep—or unconscious. Cole saw now that she was tied in the saddle, her wrists to the horn, her ankles to the cinch rings. It was sight of her that carried Cole through. In another fifty feet Partridge would be directly opposite him. With a hand and arm that seemed leaden and clumsy, Cole reached for his gun. And now Fate gave her last sardonic sneer. There was no gun!

For a moment Cole's mind refused to accept this stunning fact. He twisted his head—looked down. His blood-shot eyes verified what his clawing hand had told him. The holster at his hip was empty. Somewhere during that last mad scramble through the brush above the cliff face—or during his descent and subsequent fall, he had lost the gun!

Automatically, Cole's eyes searched the ground about him. No gun. He felt of the holster again. No gun. The fact pounded at his consciousness. No gun. And now Partridge was even with him—less than a score of feet away.

At that moment Cole Bridger went mad. He went lurching, crashing forward, bursting through the fringe of brush like a wounded grizzly on a final, dying rampage.

Horses weary, almost exhausted, threw up heads which had been low-hung and panting. They reared back—snorting, the pull of their lead ropes jerking Partridge almost off his feet. The man saw Cole, his eyes going wide and stricken. This stumbling, lurching apparition which burst from the brush at him, a feral snarl on its lips, seemed more animal than man. Partridge could not understand—could not grasp the reality of it all.

When he did recover enough to snatch at his gun, the time had been cut too short. He saw that wild figure catapulting upon him. He drew then, whipping the gun up. But Cole's driving shoulder went in under the gun, in under the stab of flame and reaching lead.

The impact knocked Partridge backward down the slope. He struck hard and a clawing fury lit upon him. Back on her horse, Norma Raine's head jerked up. She stared, through unbelieving eyes. "Cole!" she cried. "Oh, merciful God—Cole!"

But Cole did not hear. He was conscious of nothing except that here beneath him, under the clutch of his reaching fingers, was the throat of his long sought quarry. Those fingers set—sank in, grinding deeper and deeper like withes of relentless steel. . . .

It seemed ages later to Cole that he became conscious of someone crying his name over and over. And he became conscious of something else. Beneath him lay a limp dead thing—a thing twisted and still that long ago had ceased all movement. And he found that his hands were locked and aching—locked so tight that he could only withdraw them one finger at a time. But he freed them at last and got to his knees.

The agony in his back and shoulders hit him anew. That fall—it must have broken something, else that terrible, dead pain would not rack him so.

With slow clumsy movements he found his feet. He turned and looked back up the slope. There was Norma, still in the saddle. Tears were flooding her wan little face, and her eyes were pools of desperation and horror and relief.

"Cole! Oh—Cole!"

What Cole meant for a smile was merely a wooden grimace. God! How his back hurt.

"Get down, honey," he mumbled thickly. "Yuh're safe now. An' I'm—about done for."

What was that she was saying? That she couldn't get down—that her wrists were tied and her ankles were tied? Sure—that was right. Of course she couldn't get down. She was tied into that damned saddle.

Well, he'd have to be quick about getting her free. There wasn't much left for him to go on. He was nearly done—damn near done.

In a queer death-like dream Cole got back up that

slope. He got to her horse, leaned against the gaunt brute's shoulder. His hands, clumsy as clubs, picked and fumbled at that damned rawhide withe that bound her chafed and aching wrists. He did not know that she was leaning above him, her tears wetting the grimed tawniness of his bared head.

Those knots were stubborn. But he'd get 'em loose if it was the last thing he ever did. And finally he did get them loose and her hands were free.

And then, because this last act seemed to have broken the final thin barrier between consciousness and darkness, he slipped limply down into that darkness, to rest and relief from the pain that racked him.

XVII

FROM THE TIME WHEN COLE BRIDGER RELEASED HER hands, and then slumped to the ground unconscious, a good half hour passed before Norma Raine got entirely free from the saddle. Her horse, exhausted as it was, stood quietly enough, but the long stricture of that buckskin thong that had tied her wrists, had made her hands into numb, useless clubs. Her fingers would not move and her efforts at untying her ankles were futile.

Desperately she beat her hands against the saddle fork, doubling and massaging them against the smooth, hard leather. At first there were no results. Then circulation began to return. The first agony of this made her sob outright, but she knew that after this torture, strength would return. And at length it did return and, though her movements were clumsy and painful, she at last got her ankles free.

Because of the protection of her boots, her ankles had not suffered from stricture the way her wrists had, and she was able to walk immediately, albeit somewhat clumsily.

She went straight to Cole. He lay on his side, his face pillowed on one outthrown arm. She caught her breath at the gaunt, twisted expression on his face. Deep lines of fatigue and suffering bracketed his lips. But he was alive. She caught him by the shoulders and tried to ease his position somewhat. He moaned slightly.

She could do little toward moving him. Her strength was not great enough. So she did the next best thing. She brought up the pack horse and removed its burden. She arranged a pad of blankets beside Cole's sprawled figure and rolled him on to them. Then she covered him with other blankets.

The pack horse, when she freed it, moved slowly off along the line of cliff some fifty yards, then turned and pushed through a fringe of underbrush. A few minutes later it emerged, its muzzle wet and dripping. Water was in there—a spring of some sort.

The sun was just about to set. Bred to the west, Norma did the sane, practical thing. She made camp right on the spot. She found matches in Cole's shirt pocket and built a campfire. There was a small, smoke-blackened, battered cook kit in the pack and with these she prepared something to eat. She got water from the spring and made a pot of black, scalding coffee. Some of this she got between Cole's set lips. And this brought him back to a semblance of consciousness. He mumbled a few disjointed words, then sank back again into the coma of fatigue and shock.

Very grave and pale-faced, Norma ate a hurried, frugal meal. And then, in the last fading moments of daylight she set about gathering a pile of dry wood together. In her search for fuel she came across a dead pine, which had fallen before some mountain storm. The crush of branches and pitch-filled trunk gave her an idea. No doubt, far down in the country below her, now blanketed by the murk of gathering night, there would be riders, men like Jim Early and Lon Sheer—searching—searching. What better guide to them than fire!

She built a heap of dry pine needles at the edge of that fallen tangle and touched a match to it. It caught with a rush and, within ten minutes a great pillar of crimson flame licked at the sky. There was no danger of a general conflagration. The fire might spread a little, but there were too many stretches of barren rock slopes and slides for it to burn far.

Back beside her own smaller fire, Norma took the last blanket, wrapped herself in it and lay down to await the passing of the long hours of the night. Somehow she knew that what Cole Bridger needed most was rest and on her last examination of him, he seemed to be sunk in a deep sleep.

There was a certain grisly horror about this spot however. For, not fifteen yards down the slope from where Cole lay, was a dead man, staring with blank eyes at the mocking stars. It was not a pleasant thought, facing the slow, cold watches of the night with a dead man holding guard.

But Norma found little chance to ponder on this fact. Weariness exacted its toll on her also and, though she made a valiant effort to keep awake, the warmth of her fire and blanket worked its insidious way with her. She nodded again and again, then curled up in a little heap and slept also.

The crisp light of a new sunrise was in her eyes when she awoke. And a long, ringing shout echoed in her ears. She struggled to her feet, for a moment bewildered and dazed. Then she saw them—three riders, circling from that far shoulder of the mountain, around the rim of the basin toward her. Her heart leaped as she identified them. Jim Early, Lon Sheer and Mig Almada.

She waved to them, her own cry of welcome breaking off into a flood of relieving tears. And when they swung down beside her she crept into Lon Sheer's arms and cried like a child.

"Now, now, honey," comforted the grim old Texan. "Ain't a thing for yuh to cry about. Everythin's fine, now that we've found yuh. An' Cole—ain't that Cole under those blankets?"

Norma nodded. She told the story brokenly—told of that terrific day of flight and how, in what seemed some miraculous manner to her, Cole Bridger had managed to get in ahead and, with nothing but his bare hands to battle with, had ended the trail for Jay Partridge.

"Cole—hasn't been shot," she ended. "But he is hurt somehow. I—I don't know what it is. I couldn't do much with him. He was so heavy. I managed to get blankets around him and, as he seemed to be sleeping, I let him rest."

Mig Almada was already beside his beloved boss. Jim Early and Lon went over. Between them they examined him carefully. Cole still seemed in a heavy sleep. They tried his arms and legs.

"Nothin' broke," said Jim Early. "An' he ain't been hit on the haid. I don't savvy this."

"We must look closer," insisted the faithful Mig. "Help me get his shirt off."

And when Cole's torso lay bare then they understood. His back and shoulders was one great, angry bruise.

"*Dios!*" murmured Mig. "He fell—somewhere— somehow. For this we must have heat—much heat."

Under Mig's directions Jim and Lon built the fire up and placed a number of rocks in it. Near at hand Mig located a good-sized cavity in the breast of a rock slope. This he cleaned out and filled with water from the spring. When the rocks in the fire were white hot they were slithered to the water and dumped in. Shortly the water began to steam. Into it Mig plunged several of the blankets. And then, wringing these steaming compresses out, Mig laid them on that great bruise.

Faithfully he and Lon and Jim kept at their efforts. Norma helped where she could. Before long they got a definite reaction. Cole began to mumble. Several times he moaned slightly. And then his eyes opened.

Blank they were at first. Then they cleared and dawning recognition shone in them. He managed a twisted grin.

"Reckon I ain't in hell after all," he muttered. "But shore, I been teeterin' on the edges of it."

Mig smiled his gentle, sunny smile. "From now on the blankets get hotter, Señor Cole. Hang on to yourself, cowboy."

Mig did not let up in his efforts until Cole could move his arms and shoulders again. Then the faithful Mexican found a level spot close below the cliff where he hollowed out a spot and lined it with armfuls of springy bough tips and leaves. Over these he spread dry blankets. They carried Cole up and laid him carefully down.

"You will be as good as new, one of these days, señor," grinned Mig.

"I'm feelin' chipper already," nodded Cole. "My back an' shoulders ain't all daid an' useless like they were. I thought my back was busted though, when I fell comin' down that chimney."

Mig and Jim and Lon held a short conference. "I will stay here weeth Cole," said Mig. "You boys can go back to take word that all ees well, an' then return weeth horses an' more food. Eet will be a good week before Cole is able to ride again. You can take the señorita weeth you."

To this proposal Norma flatly put her foot down. "I'm staying here—to nurse Cole," she declared. For she had asked about her father and was told that aside from an aching head and a condition of wild anxiety about her safety he was as good as ever. "The one thing Dad needs more than anything else is just to know that I'm safe. You boys will make better time getting down without me along. And, my place is here, beside Cole."

In the end they agreed and, after lingering only long enough to scratch out a shallow grave for final disposal of Jay Partridge, they rode away.

The next couple of days were taken up mainly by sleeping and resting on the part of Cole and Norma. The faithful Mig seemed tireless and he knew a thousand and one tricks of native ingenuity to bring some semblance of comfort out of their wild surroundings. He brought in a huge supply of firewood. He slipped away and shot a deer to replenish their frugal commissary. He cared for the horses, locating patches of forage for them. And he was a capital cook.

Twice each day he worked on Cole's back and shoulders, rubbing and massaging them gently with some queer, black ointment he had brewed from the leaves and roots of various herbs he gathered.

"Ain't he a wonder?" drawled Cole, when, toward the end of the second day, Mig had just finished one of these ministrations and gone to bring in the horses again for the night.

Norma, sitting cross-legged beside Cole, nodded. "He is very faithful to you," she answered quietly. "You seem to have that quality about you, Cole Bridger—the quality of inspiring faith and respect."

Cole grinned. "What'cha tryin' to do, young lady—string me?"

She looked at him, very gravely, her eyes fathomless. Cole thought he had never seen her so lovely. The shadows of dread and weariness were gone from her face now. The golden tint was back in her cheeks.

"Mig told me about the Half Diamond R—our ranch, being burned," she said, abruptly switching the subject. "Do I look like a homeless waif, Cole?"

Cole shook his head. "Not to me, yuh don't. I got a home, which means that you an' yore daddy got one too. When we get back to the Punchbowl Hills, yuh're comin' to live with me."

She colored faintly. "Meaning by that, sir?"

"Yuh know darned well what I mean," growled Cole, reaching out and seizing one of her hands. "Layin' here, not able to do anythin' else but think—well I been thinkin'. There ain't no sense in yore dad goin' to all the expense of a new set of ranch buildin's. His range is still there an' his cattle are too. But his range an' mine joins. We'll just form a partnership an' run the whole business together."

"And where do I fit in?"

"Yore memory must be awful bad," chided Cole.

"Mine is different. I can remember mighty easy that I kissed you—once, back in Ezry Hoskins' store. Seems to me I told you somethin' then. Didn't I? Answer me."

She was looking at the ground, her lips twitching faintly. "Seems to me you did," she murmured, mimicing his tone and drawl. "Yes, it seems to me you did. What about it?"

"Plenty. Yuh're goin' to marry me an' boss the whole combine, that's what."

She looked at him now, a little mistily. "That sounds—like a pretty good idea." And she bent swiftly toward his reaching lips.

A ringing shout echoed across the slope.

Norma jumped to her feet. Swinging around the curve of the mountain was quite a cavalcade of mounted men. And one of them was her father.

Like a deer she ran toward him. "Dad! Dad!"

Bill Raine's hungry arms took her in. The rest of the riders came on, leaving the two together. Cole grinned up at a circle of old friends and companions.

"Hi, you roughnecks," he greeted. "Ain't yuh a long way off yore range?"

"How about yoreself, you wanderin' lobo?" retorted peppery little Pat Ryan. "Jim an' Lon been tellin' us things about you."

"Yuh don't want to believe all those two pelicans tell yuh," chuckled Cole. "Outside of an Irishman, a Texan is the biggest liar in the world."

Pat cackled joyously as he wrung Cole's hand. "You win, cowboy."

Bill Raine came up and shook hands silently. But his eyes bespoke his gratitude.

"How are things shapin' up down on the home range?" Cole asked.

"It's pretty well fumigated," said Raine. "We paid a pretty heavy price, but I reckon we've learned somethin'. It'll take a faster worker than Partridge was to catch us off our guard again."

"Some things hurt," said Cole gravely—"such as findin' that Orcutt was in with Partridge."

"It does," nodded Raine. "Orcutt was a rotten skunk. He was the one who killed Tim Harding."

Cole stared up at the old ranchman. "Bad as that, eh. He was a dawg. How did yuh find that out?"

"Oh, we caught one of their crowd. He did a lot of talkin'. Yeah, Orcutt killed pore old Tim. Shot him in the back when they were ridin' home together that night. It was a frame-up to put the daid-wood on you. Yuh see, Orcutt had one of their gang lift yore riata off yore saddle on the sly. An' after pluggin' Harding, he left the rope where it could be found easy."

"But Orcutt got nicked himself, that night."

"Orcutt did that to give himself an alibi. All he had to do after shootin' Tim was wad a bandanna over the muzzle of his gun to stop a powder burn, then bounce a shot along his laig, not too deep to be serious."

"An' Jack Batten?"

"Partridge killed him. At least, so this jasper we caught claimed."

Cole was still for a time. Then he shrugged. "There's

222

always a price to pay. We won't forget Tim and Jack—an' Sad—an' all the others. We'll take damn good care it never happens again."

Later, Cole and Raine were alone. Norma came over and joined them. "Bill," said Cole—"I want yore permission to marry yore girl. Can I have her?"

Raine grinned. "I never deny any man what he's earned. An' from the look on the faces of both of yuh, I got no say in the matter anyhow. Yuh got my blessings."

He left them there alone, while the setting sun painted the whole world in the cheery crimson of promise—the promise of better things to come.

Center Point Publishing
600 Brooks Road ● PO Box 1
Thorndike ME 04986-0001 USA

(207) 568-3717

US & Canada:
1 800 929-9108